"*Getting to Thanksgiving was no simple journey for Vince Stanford. Though he was a seasoned and successful football coach, his trip home that holiday was as challenging as any game he'd ever played. As he drove with his family to his parent's home, his reflection on his father's illness prompted a self-evaluation of his life and closest relationships. As one who recognized the importance of the faith and values instilled by his mid-western upbringing, and as one who could himself turn even a locker room into a site for value reinforcement, Vince questioned head-on what values he was passing on to his children. Ultimately, he confronted the question, "Do my kids know what I'm thankful for?" Vince's warm story finds its climax in his mother's kitchen, and her answer to the question, "What was your favorite Thanksgiving?" Her touching response will cause you to reflect personally on the meaning of this holiday that bears such significance for us all.*"

— PASTOR DOUG CLEWIS

Grace United Methodist Church, St. Augustine, Florida

"*I enjoyed it thoroughly, and the authors have a wonderful gift! Allen and Brett Bohl have captured the essence of what is important in families, schools, and communities... authentic caring relationships based on traditional family values. We need more of this powerful message!*"

—DR. JOSEPH JOYNER

Superintendent, St. Johns County School District, St. Augustine, Florida

"*In this age, where the dysfunctional family is portrayed to be the norm, it is so refreshing to be able to read of a family with parents that are still striving to pass on the torch of a legacy that was passed to them. The Sanford family is not perfect. But they share all the unconditional love, compassion, and caring that every child should be nurtured with.*"

—DEBRA SWORD

Director Community/ Economic Development, Rio Grande, Ohio

"Getting to Thanksgiving is a heartwarming story about family and faith that has readers sitting on the edge of their seats eager to read on. Vince Stanford takes his family back home for a Thanksgiving to remember. The reality of his father's illness, discovery of his grandfather's tragic past, anxiety over his sister's whereabouts, and the joy of being with family and friends leads Vince to a greater appreciation of life's simple pleasures. This encounter guides Vince to a wonderful discovery...Thanksgiving is not an annual holiday enjoyed once a year. Thanksgiving is a sense of appreciation that comes from within as we realize the shortness of life, the wonder of God's grace, and the importance of family and investing in those relationships. A fabulous book!"

—PASTOR JIM LILLIBRIDGE

Indian Run United Methodist Church, Dublin, Ohio

*"High school football coach Vince Stanford capitalizes on a family Thanksgiving trip home to reflect with his wife and two children on his own family's values, relationships and faith. An extremely enjoyable and easy read, **Getting to Thanksgiving** is another literary touchdown for co-author Dr. Allen Bohl and his son Brett Bohl. Al's Back Porch Swing set high expectations for the reader. The Bohls did not disappoint. This new heart-warming novel rivets the reader on the importance of dedication, preparation, companionship, forgiveness, friendship, determination, commitment, relationships, education, caring, values, nurturing and wise priority setting."*

—WILLIAM L. BAINBRIDGE, PH.D.

Distinguished Research Professor for the University of Dayton's SchoolMatch® Institute

Getting to Thanksgiving

1/24/09 Go BG

Al Bohl

"JD"

Published by Advantage, Charleston, South Carolina.

Member of Advantage Media Group.

ADVANTAGE is a registered trademark and the Advantage colophon is a trademark of Advantage Media Group, Inc.

Printed in the United States of America.

ISBN: 978-1-59932-056-4

LCCN: 2007939582

Advantage Media Group, P.O. Box 272, Charleston, SC 29402

Getting to Thanksgiving

Allen Bohl & Brett Bohl

Author's Disclaimer

Dedications

This book is dedicated to the memory of my dear friend, Vince Bloom, a wonderful man who cherished his family and loved the Lord. It is also dedicated to Brett's brother, my son, Nathan, who has become, like his brother, a rock as a father and husband.

—Al

I dedicate this book to the memory of my cousin Shane Patrick West who passed on way too early from this earth. He was a true leader. I think of him daily and he still inspires me.

—Brett

Acknowledgements

WITH SPECIAL THANKS TO THE FOLLOWING:

(FROM AL BOHL)

Brett, I am extremely thankful and appreciative, son, to have had the opportunity to work with you on such a worthy mission. How comforting it is to be reminded that the Lord truly works in mysterious ways.

Heidi, you've become a woman in my eyes, your editing of this adventure caused me to realize just how talented you truly are. I probably should have realized that many years ago, when I walked you down the aisle or first held your baby, Susannah. There's a place in my heart where you will always remain my little girl.

Thanks must also be given to Ben Toy and John Myers at Advantage Media Group for their guidance. And a very special thanks to Ann Summer, our editor, a beautiful lady who epitomizes Southern charm.

As with my first novel, there is a driving force behind any successful journey. Mine has not changed for over four decades; the wind that fills my sails is my best friend, Sherry.

(FROM BRETT BOHL)

I thank God for all the blessings in my life. May I honor my faith in all that I do.

Dad, you are my hero and have set the example that I try to follow of honesty and integrity in everything that you do. I am very proud of the journey that we are on and look forward to making a difference in the lives of others.

Mom, thank you for all the sacrifice that you have given for the betterment of our family.

To my Nana, thank you for leading the family with your faith and for sharing with me: Jeremiah 33:3 - Call unto me, and I will answer thee, and show thee great and mighty things, which thou knowest not.

To my wife Joyce, You are my best friend and I love you. Thank you for believing in me, for giving us the gift of two beautiful children and the window of time to start my own business. You have given me the wings to fly!

Chapter 1

The house was silent. Vince was giving Melanie and the kids another half hour's sleep before he would wake them for the trip. The aroma from a pot of coffee he had made minutes earlier was beginning to seep through the downstairs rooms. Hearing the familiar dull thud against the front door, Vince walked outside into the dark to hunt in the holly bushes for the newspaper, where it usually bounced and landed every morning. A car passed, shedding enough light for him to finish his search. He was not sure whether it was his neighbor's car, but he held up the paper in greeting just in case. Glancing at the front page weather predication, Vince frowned. *High of only 40 degrees. Possible flurries. Shoot.*

Walking back into the warmth of the kitchen, Vince reached for a worn white mug—very simple in design, but with a good solid feel. It was his favorite. He glanced around the newly remodeled kitchen and smiled in approval at the refinished cupboards and old counter-tops that had been replaced with sleek, gleaming granite. Melanie said the kitchen had gained an air of sophistication as soon as they were installed. Vince still could not believe they were finally able to afford such a luxury. He thought the plain old kitchen had served the family well, but Vince gave way to Melanie's demands that it was time for a change. He had to admit that watching guests try to find the new trash can gave him a kick. After letting them search for a few minutes, he would chuckle and then pull out a drawer next to the stove, proudly showing off the hidden trash can. As a youngster, he had hated garbage duty. His parents' wood framed trash container had forever stood duty by the old Kenmore refrigerator and always seemed to be full at the worst possible moments, like when he was grabbing his football for a quick game at the park with friends.

Enjoying his second cup of coffee, Vince flipped open the paper to the sports section. The section provided little to read, which was not surprising. Big games were rarely scheduled on Thanksgiving Eve. Besides, his mind was not on the sports page.

With his favorite mug in hand, he walked into the family room and stood in front of the French doors, looking out over the backyard patio. He glanced at the swing set sitting idly in the crisp autumn morning air. Its neighbor, the tall, regal elm that provided glorious shade in the summer, now, too, appeared to be shivering in the cold. Vince thought about going home to his parent's house. *Would this Thanksgiving be the same?*

Vince grew up loving Thanksgiving. It was his favorite holiday. Thanksgiving meant football, family, and food. It also meant spirited conversation around the dinner table. Everyone contributed—sometimes all at once—to the point where no one heard anything except his or her own voice. His father could always lean forward and silence the table with a motion of his hands. His father had a habit of saying what the family needed to hear, like a pastor who seems to stare through a window to your soul during a sermon.

Vince put both hands around his mug and enjoyed the warmth. *Dad, that old hound dog. He was preaching to us and we didn't have a clue.* He smiled. *We just soaked up whatever came out of his mouth.* He took another sip. *Dad made sure he passed on what he believed was most important.* He felt a sudden uneasiness. *Am I with my children?*

Vince's dad, Banner Sanford, had worked for over forty years in the F.E. Myers factory. He had hardly ever missed a day's work. He served half of his adult life as a lay leader for the Ashland United Methodist Church. Forty-five years ago, he had married the love of his life, Lorraine. They worked together to create a good marriage and counted their blessings. While their kids were growing up, Banner was a front row regular at the kids' games. Bragging came easy to Banner, and now the neighbors knew more than they probably wanted to about the Sanfords' grandchildren.

Taking the last sip of his coffee, Vince felt the anticipation of walking through his parents' front door into the house with candles glittering, firewood crackling, and a faint hint of cloves mixed with the sweet aroma of a roasting turkey. His mother's smile and the familiar voices of family would bring joy and affirm a safe harbor.

Lorraine was the Sanford family's anchor, and she was notorious for fussing on holidays. Like a composer searching for that perfect note, she strove to prepare the supreme dinner worthy of her family's applause. *It will be harder for Mom today.*

Over an hour had passed since Vince called for his family to wake up. "Who are we waiting on?" He stood on the bottom step and roared up towards the kids' bedrooms. "Better get going!"

Melanie, scrunching gel through the last layer of her shoulder length bob, smiled when she heard his impatient shout, "Is everything in the car?" she asked sweetly.

"Been there and ready for half an hour," he grumbled.

Vince had a habit of getting uptight when he was trying to get his family to move to his beat. He did not have that problem with his football team. As head coach of the Dublin high school team, he would crack a command, blow a whistle, and the players would hustle.

Sean scrambled from the family room. He had been waiting and lounging on the couch. He was dressed for the trip in a worn pair of blue jeans and a favorite Ohio State sweatshirt. "Not waiting on me." Tall for his age, Sean had Vince's dimpled chin, honey-brown hair, and Melanie's compassionate hazel eyes. More than a few girls in eighth grade spent extra minutes checking out that striking combination.

Vince shouted up the stairs again, "Taylor, let's go." Vince's daughter had a charming smile and short blond hair that was just long enough to braid into pigtails.

"Daddy, I'm all set." Taylor's voice was as sweet and calm as Melanie's. She started down, but scurried back up the stairs. "Whoops, gotta fetch my diary." Seconds later, she joined Sean in the entry with a small pink duffel bag stuffed to capacity flung over her shoulder.

"Come on, you guys. Uncle Conrad is going to eat the last piece of pumpkin pie before we even get there." Vince flipped off the hallway light and opened the garage door. "The boat's leaving," he called over his shoulder as Melanie slipped on her other shoe and grabbed her purse.

Vince slowly backed the Jeep Grand Cherokee down the driveway. The frozen ground was covered with a soft white blanket and the melancholy sky seemed anxious to bring more snow. Vince recalled little voices of the past demanding, "Are we there yet?" He used to use his best imitation of a conductor's voice announcing to the backseat, "Two hours. We'll be there."

They passed the Morgan House, which was decorated to perfection for the holidays. The store was owned by a great family that the entire town loved. Melanie was capable of spending the better part of any day lost in the store's tranquil, charming embrace. Just yesterday, she had purchased a candelabra and had it hand wrapped by the manager to brighten Grandma Lorraine's table. Vince noticed Melanie had not glanced toward the Morgan House. She seemed lost in thought and uncharacteristically somber.

"Remind them about Dad," she whispered.

Vince looked away, rubbing his cheek as he always did when he was nervous. He massaged his solid chin. Another habit. Stubbles felt like sandpaper against his fingers.

She added, "You know. What to expect and how to act."

Vince looked over towards Melanie's soulful eyes that assured him the children would understand.

"Sean, Taylor." Vince cleared his throat. "You need to remember Grandad's not feeling like his old, lively self." His voice was precise. "Bear in mind, he loves you kids, he's excited we're coming, but might need to rest a little more." No words came from the back seat, just understanding nods captured in the rearview mirror.

Vince gripped the steering wheel, knuckles whitening. *Chemotherapy was supposed to take care of this.* He rubbed his chin again. During the past summer, a routine physical at the Ashland County Hospital had produced dreaded news for the Sanfords. Grandad Banner had cancer.

"Lord, let him recover." Vince mumbled a prayer out the driver's window. Melanie heard him. "He will, honey. He will."

Vince was thankful for having been blessed with a caring dad who had compassionately guided and instructed him through each stage of his life. Often, Banner's lessons were molded early on and then regularly reinforced so that they might be transformed into daily habits, not occasional acts.

With his heart pounding, Vince gritted his teeth. *What about me? If something happens to me, what values will I have passed on to my children? Do my kids know what I am thankful for?*

"You know what honey? You know what bothers me?" Vince continued. "If this hadn't have happened to Dad, I'd still be plugging away coaching my rear end off and never taking the time to figure out what really matters. You know? What I am truly thankful for."

"Vince, don't beat yourself up." Melanie's voice was soft. "Besides, children never think that something will happen to their parents."

Vince wanted to cry at the thought, but he controlled himself. *I am thankful. My values are who I am.* He quickly scratched his index finger repeatedly across the bottom of his nose. *My kids need to know what matters to me.*

"Did I ever tell you…" his voice strained but gained composure as he continued, "…did I ever tell you kids how much I love your mom?" Melanie's eyes seemed to question what had caused that comment at this moment.

Sean shot a slow putdown from the back seat. "Gee Dad, never knew that."

"Hey, I'm serious." Vince called over his shoulder.

"Kidding Dad, just kidding."

"How do you know I do?" Vince placed an elbow on the console and waited before asking, "What have I done to show you?"

Taylor cut in, giggling, "You two are pretty kissy, kissy on the couch in front of the TV when you think we don't see!"

Melanie laughed at her daughter's observation and winked at Vince.

"Naah, not just that," Sean said. "It's when Dad takes out the garbage, makes the coffee, lets mom sleep in. You know, atta-boy stuff like that."

Vince winked back at his front seat passenger. Melanie's dark hazel eyes, the gentle curve of her nose, and the faint scent of Chanel Number 5 triggered memories of cherished times spent alone in her arms. "Yep, that's some pretty good stuff, Sean. Now that I think of it, those things have to add up for some points."

The Jeep rambled past familiar farmland embellished with endless acres of brown soil and miles of worn wire fences, broken sparingly with an occasional wooden fence painted white. Vince pointed, "Sean, see that tractor over there?"

"The green one? That's a John Deere, Dad." Sean spoke with a degree of confidence.

"What time do you figure the farmer that owns that thing starts it up in the morning?"

"This a trick question?" Sean seemed unsure of his dad's purpose.

Vince sketched the probable life of the unknown farmer, including the strong work ethic required to plant and raise crops. "No different than your mom and me," he concluded. "We have to work every day or you and little Taylor back there won't have your Captain Crunch every morning."

"Wheaties, Dad, Wheaties." Sean seemed indignant. "I've outgrown the Captain."

"Hey, you know what I mean," Vince barked.

Taylor watched her brother swallow his next comment. She took full advantage of the pause in conversation. "Is teaching really hard work?"

Melanie did not wait for Vince to answer. "You bet." She lowered her voice as if in a classroom, alerting everyone to stop what they were doing and listen. "Taylor, much of a teacher's work goes unnoticed, a great deal like the farmer's. We love eating his corn, but we're not with him in the spring when he plants the seed, nor in the summer when he fears his crops aren't getting enough rain. A caring teacher prepares lesson plans when no one is watching. A teacher figures out how to reach and touch each student." Melanie lifted her eyebrows. "Often working well after the school buses have returned to their barn." She playfully poked Vince's arm "Now, I don't know about this guy. They pay you for teaching study hall?"

Sean rallied for his father. "Mom, Dad's a great history teacher." He added with a sense of personal pride, "and the best head football coach in the state."

"I knew I liked that boy!" Vince smiled into the rearview mirror then pulled into a gas station. "Better fill up before we get on the interstate."

Stepping into the cold crisp air made Vince's skin tingle. The smell of gasoline crept into his nostrils while he slipped the American

Express card into the empty slot. *Talking about this stuff has to help, but, boy. . .* He took a deep breath, looked at the gas meter, and then rubbed his hand through his hair. *There sure is a lot to cover.*

Passing on life lessons and values could not be secured in a two-hour ride. Banner's efforts had taken years. Nevertheless, it sure felt good, sort of like giving a test, to examine with his children what meant so much to him. What caused him to give thanks.

Sean was the first back to the car. He looked at the gas pump. "Wow! Thirty-five bucks. Must have been a thirsty old thing."

"Good thing they pay those study hall teachers." Vince screwed the gas cap back on. "Hey, I appreciated the kind support earlier." He threw an arm around Sean's shoulder. "You just might turn out all right after all."

Chapter 2

Traffic on the interstate was heavy. The Sanfords were not the only family heading over the river and through the woods to Grandmother's house. Overhead, two black clouds lost their grip on each other and reluctantly separated. The sun took full advantage of the slight opening and darted through with the precision of an all-American running back.

"Well, would you look at that!" Melanie took a sip of bottled water and smiled. "Might be a sunny day after all."

"Better be a beautiful day when we get those report cards next month," Vince glanced up at the sky. "Taylor, how are you doing in science class?"

"Mr. Bandow likes me. I'll get an A, maybe a B." A devilish grin spread across her face. She began chewing her peppermint gum irritatingly loud. "Why don't you ask Sean how he's doing in English? I heard that Mrs. Goodridge wouldn't accept a love note to Miss Sara Casey as his homework assignment."

Sara was considered the prettiest girl in eighth grade. Sean found her irresistible along with about twenty other boys in the class.

"How did you know about that?" he fired, glaring at his sister.

"It was all over school!" The purposeful smacking of her gum continued in his face. "Everybody knows!"

"Okay, now stop smacking your gum, little lady!" Vince ordered. "And your brother's love life is his own business." Sean looked out the window. His face was on fire. Vince continued, "What's important is that you both are applying yourself in school. You remember our talk about work ethic earlier?" Vince was not really asking a question and he did not wait for an answer. "Well, getting an education is the best way to make sure you can spend your life working at something you love." He checked the traffic then set the cruise control. "Look at your mom." His voice was lively. "She loves to teach."

"Doesn't have to be teaching." Years of shared conversations allowed Melanie to continue her husband's point. "Could be anything. Could be biology, history, art, English, or maybe even international studies." Melanie and Vince exchanged smiles. He remembered her first declared major at the University of Toledo had been international studies before she discovered a passion for elementary education.

"Your mom's right," Vince said with a sturdy voice. "The main thing is to get a good education. Education's a sword, a weapon you can use to protect yourself and your future. It primes you to handle whatever gets thrown your way." Vince nodded his head. "Education is power."

Driving north, the landscape changed little. Fields were still covered with snow. Having sacrificed most of their leaves, the trees stood silently bracing for winter's assault. House after house appeared to be providing warmth and contentment for its occupants. Their chimneys released trails of smoke that dissipated without fanfare into the crisp November air.

Vince caught Sean's steady gaze in the mirror. He was still curious about what Miss Taylor Tattle-Tail had revealed. "You have a little love fumble, boy? Did Mrs. Goodridge like your sentence structure?"

Taylor giggled as she watched Sean squirm.

"Some friend Doug turned out to be," Sean puffed. "Probably still laughing. Took him all of ten seconds to read it. Then he fought me off and handed it to Butch." He hissed on, "And Butch told Mrs. Goodridge he found something."

Vince countered, "I guess if it had been Doug's note you would have given it back to him?"

"Well, I might have."

"Yeah, right," Taylor blurted under her breath.

"We'll never know for certain what you might have done," Vince soothed. "But don't give up on your friends. I've found that friends like teasing their friends." His eyebrows rose. "Doesn't mean they don't care." Shifting his weight, trying to ease his chronic back pain, Vince continued, "When times are darkest, the guy who shows up to help is a friend. When everyone else runs away, the person who stays is a friend." Putting both hands on the steering wheel, he nodded. "No doubt about it. A good friend is a wonderful gift."

"Dad's right about friends, but don't forget about your enemies," Melanie warned.

"You kids might not realize how your mom has protected my backside," Vince tapped Melanie's hand. "Being a head coach, well, means people are with you, win or tie. Losing, or making some tough calls will…"

"Create enemies." Melanie finished his sentence. "Have I had to watch out for the big guy? You bet." Her voice was adamant. "How many times have I heard, 'Why did we run that play? Why doesn't my son play more? Don't you think my son should be the quarterback? Sanford's play calling was terrible tonight!" Melanie paused. "Do I need to go on? Most people probably didn't know I heard them. Some Assho…."

"Melanie!" Vince cut his wife off. This was one subject that always raised her blood pressure, but he rarely heard her swear.

She took a long time to reply. "Well, there have been some jerks. They didn't even care if I heard them." Throwing back her head, Melanie stressed her last words. "Like I said—when it comes to your enemies…watch out, keep 'em close."

Bbbrr…Ring. "Now who's that?" Vince fumbled to answer his ringing cell phone.

"Probably some booster wanting to know why you didn't praise his son more at the banquet," Melanie quipped as she took the phone from his hand and looked down at the incoming number. "No, it's Lori," she said as she answered the phone. "Hi honey. How are you and Bonnie doing?" Melanie listened before speaking again. "We left about eight. Can't wait to see you, too. Here's your brother."

"Well, how is my favorite sister? I know, I know, you keep reminding me of that. You're my only sister." Vince chuckled. "We'll be there in an hour. Have you talked to Dad?" Vince nodded his head. "I know, I know… maybe seeing all of us will help. Well at least seeing all his girls should help." His faint grin surfaced briefly but faded just as quickly. "Glad you're on the road. We'll hold down the fort till you and Bonnie get in. Drive safe. Love you. Bye."

Chapter 3

A car sadly in need of a wash passed them on the left. Covered with slush marks, it boasted something even more disgusting to Vince: a Pittsburgh Steelers bumper sticker. "Typical Steelers fan. Can't even afford a carwash."

"Dad, at least that guy has a car," Sean ribbed. "Mom says Cleveland fans have to thumb for a ride."

"Go Steelers!" Taylor, brainwashed since she had first been dressed in an infant sized Steelers cheerleader outfit, gleefully teased her Dad.

Vince played the hurt father role well. "Unbelievable, Melanie! Look at the damage your Steelers lovin' family has inflicted on my children."

Melanie had grown up near the Ohio-Pennsylvania border, a mere sixty miles from Pittsburgh and firmly believed that if you want to see real professional football, you visit Three Rivers Stadium in the fall. Amen. "Your children?" Melanie's voice made it plain that he had crossed the line into dangerous territory. "And just after I told OUR children how I defended you." She settled back into her seat, calmly crossing her arms. "Don't you feel silly wearing those Cleveland colors?" Melanie could not hold back a slight giggle.

Vince battled. "Please don't give me that UPS and hunting joke again."

Melanie turned sideways facing him squarely. "Ok, wise guy, how do you know the driver in the dirty car hasn't fallen on hard times? Maybe he had to save, just to buy gas so he could drive his family home for Thanksgiving." She pushed her point. "His car may just be dirty from the travel."

Vince understood unconditional surrender. He lived under those terms each football season. "Three against one. I concede. Taylor, you draw up the papers. Just tell me where to sign." He looked in the mirror. "So Sean, speaking of saving, how much money have you saved for those top-of-the-line Nikes you said you wanted?"

"You had better change the subject!" Melanie appeared to care less that he had surrendered.

Sean grabbed the back of the driver's seat with both hands and leaned forward eagerly. "Twenty bucks. I was hoping you or Mom might help me out with the rest."

"Not likely," Vince quickly responded. "If you want a pair like that bad enough, you will save for them." He peeked at Melanie, hoping to see a little mercy. Observing not a smidgeon, he continued, "You have to save, son. Money doesn't grow on trees." Vince transitioned to his locker room voice, "You have to make decisions." He pointed ahead at the Steelers car. "If your Mom's right, which she is most of the time." Vince hesitated, thinking, *Maybe that'll help.* "That guy up there." Vince pointed with his head. " Probably did make a few choices about how to spend his money. I hope he did save, like your mom said, to get his family home for Thanksgiving. When you have to work for something, save for it. Then it just seems to mean more."

Melanie turned towards Sean. "Dad's right. You need to save."

Vince could not hold back a grin. *Well, what do you know? I might be back in good graces!*

"And just as important, if you don't have it, don't spend it." Melanie picked up the water bottle, took a sip, then set it down. "Let's hope Steeler man up there is not just charging things on his credit cards. That's only postponing a problem. You still have to pay." Melanie persisted, "Don't get me wrong. Sometimes credit cards are extremely important, and needed. It's knowing when to charge and when not to, but most important is knowing how you are going to pay them off. Bottom line, you need to spend your money wisely and save."

My words exactly! My words exactly! Vince silently cheered.

His cheers didn't last long as Melanie returned to the battle. "And what do you mean, the damage by my family? You want to talk about Frank?" She quickly stopped, clearly realizing what she just said. "I didn't mean it that way."

"I was kidding about your family! What am I supposed to do about Frank?" Vince asked. "You know Mom wants him there."

Melanie's voice turned soft, guilty about her ugly remark about Frank. "We could have had everyone at our place this year. You know, with Dad's situation and all. It's a lot for Lorraine."

"Are you kidding? Mom wouldn't have it any other way. Not a chance," Vince hoped he was right. "Anyways, Frank usually doesn't bother anyone."

"You're right." Melanie's response still carried her remorse. "We can all chip in and try to get Mom to let us help more."

Vince said nothing. He became preoccupied with thoughts of his mother. *Mom has really carried the load with Dad. She's been a real trooper.*

Chapter 4

They rode in silence past the next few exits. Each passenger seemed to juggle personal thoughts. Vince was organizing a couple of ideas to share, but he could not stop thinking about Frank. Vince only knew short stories about his grandfather's past. Over the years, he tried piecing things together to find out more, but the family shared little—Banner even less. When Vince pushed the subject, Banner would bristle and say, "I'm not talking about my dad. Doesn't matter, anyway." Lorraine would always head to the kitchen or pick up her knitting. What Vince did know was that somehow, alcohol and careless behavior had squandered a fortune and a beautiful farm. *How in the hell could Frank have done that? And how did Dad survive it all?*

Vince gave up trying to figure out Frank's motives for life. His thoughts wandered back to his past. His mind traveled back to Ashland, a small town positioned in the heart of Ohio farm country where he had spent his first eighteen years. Most folks in that part of America have always been well grounded. They are predisposed to work hard, attend church, cherish their families, and serve in the military when they are called. They shop with their neighbors, look forward to a good barbeque, and love high school sports on Friday nights.

Most parents in Ashland were models for their children, passing along routine behaviors and simple habits: getting up early, making coffee for the family, fixing a bowl of corn flakes, saying grace, getting a haircut every two weeks, or taking a pie over to the new family in town whom they had met for the first time in church on the previous Sunday.

How could Dad have turned out solid as a rock and not like Frank?

Ashland had experienced much change during Vince's lifetime. The farms were still there, but fewer farmers were able to make a living. Many factories remained, but the number of jobs had dwindled. Newspapers, radio, television, and now the internet brought the entire world to every family's doorstep. Many children began to question their futures. They starved for adventure and pined to see what was out there in the world. To them, leaving the confines of the known and venturing out became routine and necessary for their employment. Banner's generation, old enough that their roots were never pulled out, had only flirted with this notion. Their children were more proactive. Many attended college and then started careers hundreds of miles from home. Vince had done the same, but leaving could not diminish his love for Ashland or his childhood experiences.

As he drove along the interstate focused on the black pavement, Vince allowed special memories of Ashland to resurface.

The first memory took him back to his magical eighth grade year. His team did not lose a game in football, basketball, or baseball. He conjured up the smell of his number nine jersey fresh from the laundry, as real as ever. It lingered only for a second as he rapidly recalled that same jersey, sopping wet with mud after his last junior high football game.

His mind wandered into the high school days. He heard the crack of a bat. Memory played the video of a screaming grounder headed his way at third base. He knocked it down, reached back, cocked his arm, then threw a missile to the first baseman. His teammate's mitt snapped shut... the runner was a second too late.

No matter the sport, most of the players' parents would be in attendance. The crowd could always be counted on for some impromptu excitement. One time a mother who felt her son had been unfairly assaulted by an opponent in a basketball game as the official looked on and did nothing, instantly became a lioness protecting her cub. Fingers that could cuddle a baby, hold a hymnal, caress a spring flower, were now tugging firmly at the tall referee's jersey, demanding that he turn around to face her wrath. The boy's dad, nudged by several other laughing dads, quickly lifted the lioness away. The referee lived, but called a much fairer game from then on. Vince smiled at the memory.

He prized playing baseball. Might have been his best sport. Hoops was always fun; he was a decent point guard. Still, those other sports were like girls trying to flirt with him. His true love was football. Loved to hit. Loved the smell of grass and mud splattering his face mask. He loved three thousand Ashland Arrows shouting, "Defense! Defense!"

Vince had been considered a respectable running back, but defense was where he shone. Less than six feet and never more than a hundred and sixty pounds, he became a strong safety. Coaches loved his hustle, often saying, "Now that boy can hit!"

He remembered a cherished taste of success against a team from Mansfield. Rolling left, reading the quarterback's eyes, he had cut in front of a wide receiver, then intercepted the ball out of the air. The opposing quarterback, having some pretty spectacular wheels, roped Vince in like a steer on the ten-yard line, preventing a touchdown.

After the game, Lorraine could not hug her son enough. Banner, swollen with pride, pushed his son on the shoulder pads, "Dang, boy. I would have stiff armed that guy and run it into the end zone."

Vince remembered the warmth in his father's hands, the joy of hearing his laughter. *I sure hope Dad is okay.*

Banner's laughter was never more jovial than during family outings to Brookside Park. Brookside had a pool, ball fields, playgrounds, picnic areas, and plenty of green space that allowed kids to roam for hours while their parents sat at tables or in lawn chairs reminiscing about days gone by, discussing weather, projects, relatives, food, sports, or current conditions of the political scene.

"Can you believe what that President just did?"

"Did you see what they're charging for a gallon of gas?"

"Football team should be decent this fall. Dover is about the only team that can beat us."

The park's best feature was the pool. When the sun was cooking, the temperature swelling, the excitement of jumping into its cool, crystal clear water was a welcome relief. Conveniently located next to the pool was a quarter-mile cinder track. On a good day, none of Banner's kids could enter the pool without first running a mile. On a bad day, they had to run, then endure at least ten 100-yard sprints. Lessons in dedication, sacrifice, and determination were issued, wanted or not. Teamwork was not ignored. No family member could swim until everyone had completed their training. The first to finish always cheered on the stragglers.

Cotton mouth. Vince smiled remembering that dreaded feeling. *That same, no-good sun warmed me climbing out of the pool. Made me feel fresh, alive, like an athlete. Dang! Dad sure knew what he was doing.*

Banner's efforts with his children's running habits also accommodated a special need for Vince. Speed. If he wanted any hopes of playing football after high school, he needed to get faster. After a suggestion from his coach and support from Banner, he gave up baseball for track during the spring of his junior year. In his first meet, he was entered in the 100 meters. Looking to his left, then to his right, his brain screeched its disgust. *Do you see what I see? What were you thinking?* His hamstring twinged. *Vince! You're a fool.* The gun fired. He finished in sixth place.

Well so what if there were only seven runners? I wasn't last. Vince responded to his memory.

He never won a race, but he made a habit of knocking down his personal best times and developed enough speed to play football at the University of Toledo. The Rockets participated in Division I football in the Mid-American Conference. Vince played little and was not a star. However, that was not his goal. Proving he could step on to the field with the big boys and make a contribution was his goal.

More than Vince's football abilities were under the microscope during his collegiate years. Eighteen years of life's lessons were exposed, confronted, appraised, and tested.

Vince scanned the Jeep. Taylor was writing in her diary, Sean was catching a few winks, and Melanie was flipping through the pages of her latest *Southern Living* magazine. He allowed himself to be overwhelmed with a spirited flow of emotions.

Friends, sacrifice, drinking, love, leadership, teamwork, study habits, values, manners. He exhaled a deep breath. *You name it… I faced it, did it, or tried to avoid it.*

He sighed.

Melanie heard him. "You okay, honey?"

Sheltering where his mind had led him and feeling a bit embarrassed, he answered. "Sure, just thinking." He knew those words would draw another question.

"What were you thinking about?" Melanie asked, trying to straighten her wrinkled skirt.

"Oh, nothing, just getting hungry, I guess," he offered. Then he added, "Well, actually, I was remembering how beautiful you were back in Toledo."

"Oh, stop it." Melanie patted his cheek and then went back to her *Southern Living.*

Chapter 5

Melanie and Vince discovered each other at The University of Toledo. She was the gorgeous brunette sitting in the front row in Psychology 101. Sporting a deep tan, she looked like someone who had spent the weekend on Key West. Her charming smile and slender body made Vince guess that this beauty could be one of those models walking down the runway in a fashion show.

The weather had been nice the spring they first met. It taunted Vince and his love of golf. He was a Jack Nicklaus wannabe and thus he challenged the record for missed class time. Vince found it easy to sacrifice his academics for a beautiful golf course with lightening-fast greens. Melanie, on the other hand, had perfect attendance.

After class one dreary rainy day, Vince mustered up enough courage to introduce himself. He really wanted to meet Melanie, but also knew he could use some assistance with the class, especially by way of her class notes. As the professor dismissed them, he quickly jumped from his back row seat and rushed up front. Melanie was snapping her backpack shut.

"Hi, I'm Vince. Vince Sanford." His voice caused her to turn. "You got a minute?"

"Sorry, I got to go. I'm late for work." Melanie's 'sorry' was forceful. "You don't come to class much do you?"

Ouch! Rejection.

Later in the quarter, the professor, who went by the nickname of "Ace", was giving a grand lecture about how hard it is to maintain enthusiasm over an extended period of time. Ace set a challenge. "I'll pay someone ten bucks if they can stand in front of the class and be enthusiastic for one minute...a straight 60 seconds." There were no takers. Vince calculated, *Ten bucks. The green fees are only fifteen!* He accepted the challenge.

Vince gathered himself, walked up next to Ace, and then enthusiastically sang the Toledo fight song. The class was pumped and gave him an ovation. He won Ace's ten dollars and collected an even more noteworthy prize—Melanie's attention. The singer had finally earned a bona fide date.

Like a lot of young college kids, Vince struggled though his first two years. He fell in with some pals who were not genuine friends. They were the kind who knew about underage drinking, but still bought drinks. The kind who would not hesitate to let you drive drunk. The type who placed partying way ahead of studying. Doing the right thing was rarely discussed.

A stream of cars traveling well over the speed limit started to pass the Jeep on the left. Vince did not try to join them. He squeezed the steering wheel. *Alcohol!* He frowned into the front windshield. *Dang Alcohol. Why was it the only time that I got in trouble, alcohol was involved? It was always the common denominator.*

He glanced over at Melanie with loving gratitude. *What a tremendous influence in my life. She made a difference. Frank must have never had anyone like her.* Thoughts of Frank reappeared. *This Thanksgiving I'm going to make that son of a gun talk. He's not going to just sit there on the couch.* Feeling confident, his mind returned to college days.

When he fell in love, Vince found himself spending less time with careless friends. He gained new ones, and stopped the habit of drinking for entertainment.

His time on the football field also progressed. He was in better shape than ever and was a starter on specialty teams. He loved his teammates. A few had the ability to play pro football, while most, like Vince, recognized Toledo would be the end of their playing days. Character and integrity, not talent, determined their friendships. They came from diverse backgrounds: rich, poor, ethnicity, religion. It did not matter. What did matter was whether or not the team could count on you. Being able to count on Vince was never an issue. He always put the team before himself and his teammates noticed. *I miss those guys.*

Vince sat up in the driver's seat. He wiggled a little bit, trying to comfort his aching back. "Hey, you remember me telling you about the days I played football at UT?"

"Are you kidding, Dad?" Sean said. "Only about a hundred times."

"I was a walk-on," Vince paid no attention to his son's response. "Wasn't a star. Everyone had a role." Rubbing the back of his neck, he continued. "Playing in a good program means you won't be the same as when you started." Vince nodded his head, slowly. "What matters is making an effort. Making a contribution. Making the team better."

Melanie had been listening. "I loved watching Number 31 storming down on those kick-offs. Bet there's a few Bowling Green Falcons still running around with headaches from those days."

Vince appreciated knowing he had been a big-time player in her eyes. He looked into the mirror. "You know, you learn a lot from football." He dropped his eyes back to the road. "Preparation, organization, staying in the moment, the importance of playing the next play."

"Dad, you learn that stuff in other sports, too." Sean added with a voice that suggested he was becoming a well-rounded athlete in his own right.

"Absolutely! Why do I like the two of you to play golf? You have to be honest, be respectful, and go by the rules. If the ball moves…"

"I know," Sean interrupted. "You gotta count the stroke." Everyone in the car knew they had heard that one at least a thousand times.

Taylor and Sean had been encouraged to be involved with a wide range of sports. Sean was on the middle school football team, basketball team, and in the spring he golfed. Taylor was just as active. She played soccer, basketball, and, like her brother, swung the clubs.

Melanie was also no stranger to competition. She had been more than a fair high school basketball player and had regularly won events in track. Those experiences had groomed her well for the life of a coach's wife and mother of children who loved participating in sports.

Vince had coached Sean's first basketball team and was now coaching Taylor's. Cherishing the assignment, he loved watching the youngsters develop their skills and relished teaching them the fundamentals. He wished for nothing more than to just watch them compete, knowing they were learning discipline and gaining self-confidence. Melanie seemed to enjoy his coaching youngsters for an additional reason. She told the parents, "It's kind of neat to watch the high school football coach work on his patience."

The interstate traffic was hustling. Melanie inserted her favorite *Journey* CD. Vince turned slightly and asked over the music, "Sean, how's basketball practice going? You guys ready for your first game?"

"We're gonna be good, Dad. Ryan looks solid and you know Hector can play."

"Well, that's good." Melanie said. "I know someone in this car who can just twinkle her eyes at the coach and get to play as much as she wants."

Taylor snapped her diary shut. "Mom!" She pushed the back of the seat. "Dad, tell Mom I can shoot. That's why you play me."

"Practice starts in a few weeks, honey. We'll let your mom come out and see if she can beat you in Around the World."

"Let me know when!" Sean was excited. "Give me a piece of that action."

"Well, well, Mom," Vince chuckled. "You've got some competition." Melanie's face glowed, thoroughly amused.

Vince monitored a semi passing him on the left. "You would think those drivers would be worried about getting a ticket." He shook his head and then continued his sports talk. "You know, it's not just the playing. It is all that intangible stuff that I always appreciated." His voice deepened. "Having to be on time, following directions, learning to sacrifice, getting along with people." He stopped as if to catch his breath. "You know what I mean, Sean and Taylor?"

"Sure, Dad," Taylor said. She had stopped chewing her gum in respect.

They'll come to be thankful for those experiences, like I did. Sports have molded my life.

Chapter 6

Vince began coaching in Ottawa Hills right after college and his summer wedding to Melanie. The school system hired him to teach History and to be an assistant football coach. The principal also asked him to help coach track, which meant another five hundred bucks. He agreed. Track had helped him gain a little speed back in high school and now in his first job, it was going to help earn a little extra cash. Melanie found out she was pregnant before the team played their first football game, so that additional money came in real handy.

The Village of Ottawa Hills sat on the western edge of Toledo. The streets were lined with one beautiful home after the other, each competing for architectural splendor. Every season was gorgeous in this community, but fall claimed the star season. The radiant oaks and maples that lined each street displayed brilliant foliage well into November.

Unable to afford a home in the village, Vince and Melanie rented a two-bedroom apartment off of Bancroft Street near the university. During this time, they learned to depend on each other and fell deeper in love. Awaiting their first born, the couple learned how to do without, shopped sparingly, and enjoyed cheap entertainment.

Parking downtown, alongside the Maumee River cost nothing. Over the water, they would watch the golden sunsets as passengers in various sized yachts and boats leisurely traveled back and forth from Lake Erie. The water explorers seemed to be very privileged characters from a novel or famed movie. Vince and Melanie would cuddle close in their car, hold hands, and dream that someday someone might actually invite them to jump on board.

In the early coaching years, attending church was difficult. Melanie did not like going to church alone and Vince was obligated to run over to the school for Sunday morning preparation meetings. The coaching staff, eager to get ready for the next game, did not want to waste time. He understood coaching responsibilities, but missing Sunday service still gnawed at him.

Banner and Lorraine had made sure all of their kids attended church regularly. Every Sunday morning at 10:30, Banner would issue his order: "Time to go," and the car would head to the Ashland United Methodist Church. Returning home after an hour in the pews was particularly delightful. As the family entered through the back door, the irresistible smells of dinner slow roasting in the oven always welcomed them.

When coaching demands lightened, Vince loved going home to his parents for the weekend and attending church service. He would always sit with Melanie in the same pew he had wiggled on as a youngster; the same one his family had claimed as their own for over two decades.

During their weekend visits, Lorraine made everyone feel like it was a special holiday. Pies were baked, cinnamon rolls prepared, a huge ham or turkey was in the oven, and there were always plenty of Vince's favorite, green beans. The family would spend the evening sitting around talking with relatives and neighbors or playing cards. Rook and gin rummy were the favorites. Lorraine would start a pot of coffee and then offer refills as desserts were passed around a second time. Frank rarely attended these weekend visits. When he made an appearance, he spent most of his time on the living room couch glued to the TV, never involved in any of the conversation or games. *He never cared to connect with any of us.*

Leaving on Sunday evening was never easy. Kisses and hugs were shared all around. Then Banner and Lorraine would stand on the front porch and give one last affectionate wave. Vince would honk the horn, providing the signal that the weekend was officially over, their goodbyes real. *Lord, how I cherished going home. I pray Sean and Taylor will feel the same.*

Once the rusting blue Plymouth Duster would arrive back at their apartment in Toledo, Vince would be back to the grind. He would carry in the suitcase, check the answering machine, and then head to the kitchen table to complete lesson plans for the following week.

Anyone would attest to the fact that Vince was an excellent teacher. He brought history alive in his classes by performing like Abe Lincoln, Robert E. Lee, or Ulysses S. Grant. If someone knocked on the door, the students would look to see if it was Stonewall Jackson or General Sherman asking for his next orders. People like Martin Luther King, Woodrow Wilson, or Eleanor Roosevelt jumped off the pages and became real people to his students. His goal was not to just have his students learn names, places and facts, but to know how places, people, and events shaped the past so the future had a chance of being better. Vince never failed to remind them that, "History will repeat itself. The trick is knowing how to get the best repeat!"

His teaching methods carried over to the practice field and were most effective in his coaching. The running and defensive backs were his responsibilities. The head coach, Bob Covington, gave Vince a lot of room. He would tell Vince, " Just don't have them running the wrong direction and don't get beat deep."

Vince always sought perfection and knew it would never happen, but he was still as stubborn as a bull. His voice shouted regularly, "We are staying here until we get it right." The running backs would run the same play over and over, do endless fumble drills, and then run sprints till their hearts thundered against their ribs. At first the players hated it, but then they shaped new feelings for Vince because he coupled strict training with hugs.

If one of his players showed great effort and character whether he was a starter or not, Vince would give praise like the youngster had just won a Heisman. He would give a smile that could warm on the coldest day. For those most needy, Vince would give them a hug and let them know they were worth something. They were special. By mid-season, no player had gone the wrong way, gotten beat deep, and the team had not one fumble. The running and defensive backs were believers and would literally run through a brick wall for Coach Sanford—or at least bounce off trying.

The players loved when Melanie would drop by practice with Sean. Melanie would sit on the first row of the bleachers with Sean propped up in his stroller. During water breaks, a few players would always run over to say hello. Sean got greetings like, "Tell your dad not to run us so much," or "Hey, little man, how you doing?"

Vince would shout, "Hey, let's go!" and Melanie would happily give the players a hand slap as they scurried back to their coach. Instinctively, the coach and his wife would pause and share a smile with each other.

At the end of the year Vince and Melanie, regrettably had to say goodbye to the young players. The coach had been offered a new job.

One of Coach Covington's buddies was head football coach at Vermilion High School and wanted Vince to join his staff. A chance to work at a bigger school justified his acceptance; however, the dollars and cents of the change truly secured the move. He'd be making five thousand dollars more a year, a fortune to him and Melanie at the time. Melanie was offered a first grade teaching position, and Vince would fill a high school history vacancy.

Located on Lake Erie about eighty miles east of Toledo, Vermilion looked like a quaint New England village. In a loving but sneaky way, Vince knew the move would certainly aggravate his Pittsburgh Steelers' loving wife to be moving into the heart of Cleveland Browns country. Another plus was that Ashland was a mere forty miles south on Route 60.

Vince and Melanie rented a small home in Orchard Beach on the outskirts of town. The house had been built in the 1930s as a summer cottage, but had been winterized in the 50s with a fuel oil furnace system for year-round use. Nestled one block from the lake, summer breezes drifted through the screened windows, providing welcome relief during hot summer days. In the winter, Vince had to constantly monitor the fuel oil tank. Those pleasant breezes were nowhere to be found in February.

Melanie especially liked the front porch. It was a perfect place to gather. It provided spectacular views of the lake. Family visited year round, but mostly in the summer. The thought of splashing around in

Lake Erie seemed to always warrant sufficient motive for checking up on the young coach and his wife.

Vince found the home right after his interview for the job. He liked it immediately. The next weekend he drove Melanie over to Vermilion so she could get a good look at the property and make her assessment. When she first saw the beautiful view of Lake Erie, her smile beamed. When she looked across the road her smile changed to that of someone who had just caught her child in the cookie jar. Melanie was looking at the Vermilion Country Club.

At this point in his career and with a new baby, Vince had little time to golf. Sean had been an easy delivery for Melanie and other than a rash once in a while, the baby was in perfect health. But this was not college. Vince understood and accepted that his job and family trumped his love for any sport. Melanie clearly understood her husband's affection for the golf. She simply squeezed his hand, "Vince, I do hope you get to play some."

Their first year in Vermilion was filled with all the ups and downs associated with moving to a new town and starting a new job. As in Ottawa Hills, Vince earned immediate respect, becoming a hit with both players and students. The football team lost two games during the regular season and just missed getting into the state playoffs. Melanie loved being able to teach, but dropping Sean off at the nursery school every day was difficult. Each morning before leaving him with the nursery attendants, she would give her son a hug then kiss him once on his forehead. She would walk to her car with a forced smile, blocking away the tears and her heartache.

Sean's nursery school was actually a wonderful choice. Melanie had done her homework. It was held in the basement of the Evangelical and Reformed Church on Grant Street. After checking out several references, Melanie encouraged Vince to meet the minister, Reverend Bradstreet. They decided to invite him over for coffee and dessert. Melanie was nervous; Vince was not. Any time there was a good reason to enjoy some of Maxwell's best coffee and more than his fair share of Melanie's peach cobbler, his attitude was easy to predict: "Count me in."

During his visit to the Sanfords' house, Bradstreet wowed them. He was a slender man with dark hair, penetrating eyes, and a perpetual smile. He shared with them his faith in the Lord and his commitment to help people find life through Jesus Christ. "The people who serve our church are dedicated to doing the same," explained Bradstreet.

Melanie reached over and grabbed Vince's hand, letting him know she was very pleased to hear such heartfelt words.

"You can be assured that baby Sean will be nurtured in a very caring way," Bradstreet told them.

The next Sunday Melanie and Vince were front and center in the Evangelical and Reformed Church of Christ. They joined the congregation two months later.

Dropping Sean off still hurt, but Melanie knew she had done her best to find excellent child care. The afternoon pickup was always joyful and rewarding.

Melanie had twenty-two students in her first grade class. Each one could have been Sean, because she cared for them all like they were her own. She treated them with dignity and respect while encouraging them to be responsible. A beautiful tree filled with red paper apples covered her classroom bulletin board. Each student's name was perfectly printed on an apple. Melanie placed a wicker basket under the tree, and if a student misbehaved, his or her apple would be placed into the basket. No child wanted their apple off the tree, as they all wanted Mrs. Sanford's approval.

Melanie consistently taught, explained, listened, encouraged, and hugged. Her students were nurtured, trained, and introduced to the world of knowledge. Providing the best conditions for her students to learn was always her focus.

Of all the disciplines, reading was her main passion. Melanie set a foundation for each child to be a successful reader. She cherished the thought of the day her students would find themselves "lost" in a great novel or planning their day around a book, eager to get their required tasks finished so they could enjoy another chapter.

During their second year in Vermilion, Melanie watched a new class continue to improve and Vince witnessed the same with the football program. The team made it into the district playoffs.

"Never give up! You *never* give up!" Vince had shouted, as he huddled with the players after a come-from-behind victory in their first playoff game. "Preparation, dedication, determination. That's what success is all about."

Vermilion went on to get beat in their second playoff game against Fostoria. Nonetheless, the town was proud of their team and glowed with the prospects of what might happen next season.

Vince and Melanie were aglow for an additional reason. They had just found out they were expecting another baby. As fate would have it, their second child would not be born in Vermilion. They were moving. Coach Covington had been busy bragging about his former assistant again.

Chapter 7

Vince noticed that one of his favorite Alan Jackson songs was playing on the radio. He turned the volume up, leaned back, and hummed along until he detected everyone was smiling at him. "I'm not singin, just hummin." He got nods from the back seat. "Hey! You guys remember living in New Carlisle?"

Vince had accepted his first head coaching position at Tecumseh High School located on the outskirts of New Carlisle, Ohio. Tecumseh was a big country high school, sorely in need of turning around their football program. Success, even a few wins, had been dodging them for years. The superintendent for the school system was a high school friend of Bob Covington at Ottawa Hills. Bob told his friend, "If you guys ever want to win a game, you better hire Vince Stanford away from Vermilion." So, they did.

Vince focused back on the road as two more semi trucks raced past. After shaking his head in disapproval, he took a quick peek in the mirror. Taylor caught his glance. "Sweetheart, I can still remember like it was yesterday coming to pick you and your mom up at the Springfield hospital. I knew you could shoot even back then."

"Dad, no way. I was too small."

Vince embraced the recollection of Melanie handing Taylor to him for the first time. He accepted the precious gift. Vince enjoyed his task of providing, to the best of his ability for her and her brother, while at the same time allowing them to grow into their own. Holding her in his opened palms, he thanked the Lord for guiding such a beautiful child into the world. *Two miracles. Sean and Taylor. Thank you, Lord.*

"I saw it in your hands and in your eyes." His voice melted.

Melanie added her own recollections. "Honey, your dad likes to brag about you, but what I remember is he was plain lucky to be there."

"Now, don't be telling that story again. They're going to think it's true," Vince grumbled.

"Well, it is true," Melanie assured. Her eyes sparkled in anticipation of telling a good story on Vince. "It was a hot Saturday. July the 13th. Not a cloud in the sky." She pressed her lips together, "You two know what that means?"

"Dad was golfing." Sean blurted the words out like it should be obvious to all.

"Give that boy an A," Melanie grinned. "Dad was playing with Doug Gray, the basketball coach, and Mike Weiland." Melanie hissed, "Can you believe the guy driving this Jeep?" Melanie stabbed her husband with a mischievous glare. "He called it *work*."

"Now wait a minute." Vince protested. "It **was** work. We were trying to get Weiland to raise some money for new uniforms. Are you forgetting Mike was president of the Tecumseh Boosters?"

Melanie's second glare cut him off like a judge ruling someone out of order. "*I'm* telling this story." She tapped his arm, "Like I was saying, your father was out playing around and here I was starting into labor early."

Vince's voice rose like an aggressive defense attorney. "You told me it was okay. We had the first tee time. I'd be back by noon."

"Pay no attention to him." Melanie's voice was a judge's gavel. She waved her hand, eased her voice. "It was about ten in the morning. Sean and I were watching cartoons." Taylor set her pen between the pages of her diary and then shut the book. Melanie winked at her. "I felt you kick and had a sudden cramp. It was time, so I called the golf course." Melanie gave a push on her husband's right forearm. "I will give the big guy credit. He had alerted the entire golf course staff. They drove out in a cart and brought him back to his car." Melanie's smile grew. "To this day, I'm not sure what really happened. Mr. Weiland swears your dad tried to barter by asking, "We've got two holes to play. Do you think we could hurry up and get them in?"

"Hey, we got there in plenty of time. Didn't we?" Vince was pretending like he was more interested in the landscape than the conversation.

"If you call getting to the hospital at half past noon," Melanie raised her eyebrows to stress her point, "and baby Taylor arriving just after one, plenty of time."

"Sean you were too young to remember, but it's coming back to me." Vince nodded his head with confidence. "While your Mom got to lie down in one of those big cushy beds, everybody pampering her, you and I, we headed to the waiting room." He hesitated for impact. "Two other gentlemen were already there and they were pretty bright fellows as I recollect." Vince hesitated. "I knew they were bright, be- cause they already had the TV tuned to a baseball game. It was a big one! The Indians versus the Red Sox. Your sister, Taylor, didn't even let us watch a full inning."

Taylor giggled and Melanie groaned, "Oh, please!"

"Hey, it didn't matter," Vince's voice lifted with pride. "I was holding my little girl and staring at her gorgeous mom."

"You're something else," Melanie leaned over and gave Vince a gentle slug on his right arm.

Silence resumed in the Jeep. Vince turned the heat down a notch and then put his hand back on the steering wheel while his fond mem- ories of New Carlisle returned. Melanie had found a three-bedroom ranch house on the west side of town. Her special eye for decorating caused the house to be transformed into a home of unique and delight- ful character. She spent a little more time on the kitchen. Meals they ate there were extraordinary—not because they were elaborate or im- mense—but because they had purpose and meaning for a young couple with two children. The kitchen table was for the head coach, the place where he could regularly connect with the people he cherished most.

Dinner might be as simple as macaroni and cheese with a few hotdogs, but it was always seasoned with love and care. Vince could sit with his wife, discuss a problem at school, or smile and talk with Sean and Taylor about their day. *I truly am thankful for those times. I loved gathering around that table.*

He briefly took his eyes off the road and looked over at Melanie. "What ever happened to that blue tablecloth we always used in New Carlisle?" Vince asked.

Melanie gave him a quizzical look. "The blue one?"

"Yeah, the blue one with the small yellow flowers. I really liked it."

"Honey, we haven't had that thing for years. Sold it at the garage sale when we moved to Dublin." She softly stroked the side of her chin. "Think I got fifty cents for it."

"We got screwed. I loved that tablecloth. You know, we had some great meals on that thing."

"Dad, I think I remember it," Sean offered. "Those yellow things were birds."

"Nope, honey, they were flowers like your dad said. You used to spill your Lucky Charms on top of those flowers."

"What about me? Did I eat there?" Taylor asked, not wanting to be left out.

"Your high chair was state of the art," Vince answered his daughter, then focused back on his thoughts. "Our eating together was what was important. You wonder why I shut off the TV and make us all sit at the table for dinners every chance I get?" Vince moved his hands to the bottom of the steering wheel. "It forces us to talk to each other and lets you watch my good table manners," Vince explained with a grin.

Their house in New Carlisle was near a city park with a wonderful play area for children, two tennis courts, and a full-length basketball court. In the summer after church on Sundays, Melanie would fry up some chicken, make some potato salad, and then the Sanford family would head to the park. Vince would push Sean on the swing or merry-go-round while Melanie would watch Taylor in her little stroller. The trees in the park provided refreshing shade and the birds sang to everyone visiting. People would come and go throughout the afternoon. Many were most likely resting from whatever problems the previous week had dealt them, while some were preparing for those the upcoming week would surely bring.

The basketball court at the park rarely went unused. Someone always seemed to be shooting. Pick-up games could happen in a moment's notice. The best time was in the spring after five o'clock when school was out and people were home from work. The weather was usually warm enough to work up a good sweat and by dusk as the sun set on the western horizon it was cool enough to make a cut off sweatshirt feel just right.

Playing in pick-up basketball games proved to be very enlightening. Life lessons were endless: teamwork, sharing, determination, honesty, and even humility. Learning humility did not feel good to Vince. It frequently came in the form of an opponent misusing him for three or more straight baskets. When he was forced into being humble, Vince cursed but accepted. Then he moved on.

He loved the time after the games almost as much as playing. Vince would high- five his friends, pick up his ball, and head back to the house. His cut-off t-shirt would be drenched in sweat as he walked home while the sun peeked over the maple trees, giving the last light of day. Melanie was often waiting on the front porch watching her warrior return home. As he neared the porch, Vince cherished the smile that lit up her face. She would always chide him on his performance.

"Did you let one of those ninth graders beat you again?"

He knew not to retaliate; it would only get worse. Instead he walked inside to the refrigerator, got a cold beer, and returned to sit down in the white wicker chair next to Melanie's swing and Taylor's stroller. Sean would come running from his toys in his bedroom and start dribbling the ball.

Their porch conversations were always easygoing. They would talk about school, friends, or family while Vince leisurely sipped on his beer, allowing his ragged muscles to rest. Once in a while, he would he talk about next year's football team. Vince knew that Melanie had to listen to more than her fair share during the season so he tried to spare her from overkill during the off season.

It was hard for him not to talk about football, though. His five years in New Carlisle had provided plenty of opportunities to grow as a head coach and expand his skills. Handling his success was one skill he nurtured.

The first year he won only two games, but during the next four he recorded thirty two victories while posting only eight losses. Winning was very important, but winning with class and dignity was even more important. Vince's teams were drilled to perform to the best of their abilities while acting with the utmost sportsmanship. When parents would stop by practice they would repeatedly hear Vince barking out, "You win with character. You respect your opponent." Then later on in the practice, out of nowhere he would reinforce his beliefs, "Boys, we are going to win on Friday and when we do, we're all going to smile, then keep our mouths shut. No bad mouthing. We're not bodacious, just good!" He'd slap the closest player on the shoulder pads, rub his chin, then holler, "Now let's run that play again. We're going to surprise them with this one."

Come Friday night, his teams performed with precision and never failed to display splendid sportsmanship. The fans noticed. He started receiving more positive cards and letters after games. Mike Weiland, the head of the boosters, was all smiles. Donations had doubled.

Vince practiced what he preached on the field. Win or lose, he would walk across the field to shake the opposing coach's hand and compliment several of his players. Success was never going to overshadow his integrity.

As the years went on, he actually developed a list of comments he would somehow figure a way to interject into a practice so that some virtue, some thought, was always being reinforced with his team. By the end of the season each player had heard repeatedly:

Focus, you got to stay focused!

Be prepared—better yet, be over-prepared!

Luck! When our determination connects with our preparation, the other team's going to say we are lucky!

No back stabbing! We're a team here. Somebody makes a mistake…a fumble, a missed tackle, we pick them up!

Guess what! In a few seconds they're going to snap the ball again! Another chance to make a big-time play!

Discipline, boys! Discipline!

Melanie always had the same seat in the bleachers. Carrying Taylor and holding Sean's hand, they would climb up ten rows and sit on the end, looking right down on the forty yard line. The football field was always cut to perfection as if the local barber had taken the afternoon off to perform his expertise on the green surface. White chalked lines stood out like the frame that surrounds a precious piece of art. The smell of popcorn and hotdogs drifted through the air. When colder weather hit, steam coming off a cup of hot chocolate carried by a fan heading to a seat made everyone think, "That looks really good."

By halftime, Sean always had figured out a way to make sure he had a cup.

Sean tolerated watching the game from afar, but what he waited for most anxiously was the fourth quarter. That was the time his mom would say, "You can go down now." He would fly like a bird released from its cage down the steps and on to the sidelines. Vince had a manager waiting to take Sean to the end of the bench. The manager would stand with him as Sean experienced the thrill of watching his dad's team compete. Blow by blow, one team would try to move a yard closer to the goal line. Grunt by grunt, the other team would try to prevent the other's advance. Sean especially loved when the action was directly in front of him. He would not back away, even when tugged by the protective manager. Only when he heard a bark from the head coach, "Everybody back!" did he give ground, but even then only a few feet. His eyes would sparkle as he watched an opposing receiver being pummeled to the ground by a fierce tackle. His stomach would churn when he looked inside the player's helmet and saw pain etched on his face. The defender, jumping to his feet, with a glowing smile showed no such pain. Sean would watch his dad, clapping his hands, cheering the play, "Now that's what I am talking about. What a hit!"

Sean would catch eye contact with the head coach and receive a secret wink that shouted, "I love you, son." The coach would then pull on his black cap, jerk on his headset, and quickly return his attention to the next play. After the game, the fans watched little Sean follow in the steps of his dad to the fifty-yard line. After the handshakes, Vince would pick up his son, give him a hug, and then they would head to the locker room together, hand in hand.

Once, after a tough contest, a supportive booster told Vince that he loved watching Sean follow in his footsteps to the middle of the field. "He's going to grow up just like you."

Vince smiled back with appreciation. "That's why I better always walk straight."

Melanie and Taylor would be one of the last to leave the stands. She would congratulate the parents who sat around her and let them know that their son had played a super game. She enjoyed listening to them compliment her husband, but reminded them that he did not play one minute of the game. The players had made all the difference.

Of course, it was not always a happy ending. Vince's first year, when he won only two games and they were the last two of the year, Melanie had a chance to work on her patience and tolerance. Vince did, too. He was verbally beaten up pretty badly by the frustrated fans who had been living with poor performing football teams for a decade.

Some of the statements were brutal and unforgiving. One fan even pulled the school district's superintendent into the battle. "What was that superintendent thinking? Where did they get this coach from anyways?"

His friend sitting next to him added fuel to the fire. "This fool's never been a head coach. Tecumseh needs to win and they hire some idiot with little experience."

Melanie was only five rows down and did not have to strain to hear their comments. She turned and scorched both men with her glare. One more word and Taylor's baby bag would have been flying toward their heads.

The second season started off with a bang with six straight wins, and the comments from the stands showed that the bandwagon was starting to fill.

"I knew all along this guy knew what he was doing."

"When my daughter said she liked his history class, I figured he might be okay."

"Kids say he is tough. I like seeing someone who will discipline these kids. That's why we're winning."

The best compliment came from the guy who barely escaped a head wound from Taylor's bag the year before. Suddenly, he was Coach Sanford's best friend. "Knew it all along. Vince was just an assistant waiting to be a head coach."

After each game, Tecumseh's locker room provided a place for value reinforcement. With each team member on one knee, Coach Sanford would remove his cap and speak from his heart, "The win tonight did not happen over the last two plus hours. It came from the dedication and discipline you displayed over the last nine months. It came from your work, your mental toughness, and from your courage. Let's take a moment to shut our eyes and each give thanks in your own way for this gift of success." They went on to win eight games that year and each team continued to count their blessings throughout the next three seasons at Tecumseh.

Vince stopped his reminiscing and turned his head towards Sean in the back seat then quickly back to the road, "Remember coming down on the Tecumseh football field when we lived in New Carlisle?"

"Are you kidding, Dad? I loved coming down to the field." Sean leaned forward and returned a question, "You remember when Piqua had us beat? It was the last game of the year. Only eight seconds left and we were down 21-20 and you let Roger Walker kick a field goal."

"Remember? It was a forty-nine yarder."

"He was right in front of me," Sean had to control the excitement in his voice. "The hold was good and he kicked it pretty solid."

Vince chuckled, "Yeah, we all were praying that it had enough steam to make it."

"I can still see it bouncing off the cross bar and falling over it."

"It didn't look pretty, but those officials still had to raise their arms above their heads." Vince rubbed the bottom of his chin. "That's why you never give up. You keep fighting. Nobody thought we could win that game."

Melanie added, "You two think you were the only ones who can remember that game? It was Chris Beemer who caught the pass to set up the field goal attempt."

"Chris was a good one." Vince nodded in agreement.

"And just think," Melanie laughed. "He couldn't catch a lick until wonder boy over here started coaching him."

"I'm thankful for that team, those players, that opportunity. But, what I remember most, more than Roger's kick or Chris's catch, was the Monday after. That's when we got the news about your mom." The laughter subsided.

Melanie's mom, Ruth, had been suffering with heart problems for several years. The call came early on Monday morning following the memorable Piqua game. Melanie was advised that she might want to come home. During Sunday night Ruth had felt some chest pains, so Melanie's dad, Ray, had taken her to the hospital. Throughout the night and into Monday morning, things did not seem to be going in the right direction.

Both Melanie and Vince requested substitutes for their classes and headed east to the Ohio border. When they finally arrived at the hospital, it was too late. The doctors had tried everything possible, but Ruth's condition had worsened and she had taken her last breath with Ray by her side, tenderly holding her hand.

Sean lowered his eyes "I loved going to see Nana." His voice picked up a little. "She had the softest hands and always had a big smile."

"I can't remember what Nana looked like." Taylor seemed to apologize.

"You were too little, honey." Melanie shielded her. "She loved you both dearly. Taylor, I remember Nana carrying you around to each table at the family reunion when you were only a year old, telling everyone that this was her little sunflower."

"She was mighty proud of you, pumpkin," Vince added. "I guess she liked Sean too." He smiled at his son. Sean smiled back.

"Nana loved your dad." Melanie shook her head. Vince could tell his wife was sifting through tender memories. "She'd fry him chicken, make him biscuits, and she loved to make him graham cracker crust pies."

"They were sooo good." Vince's voice left no doubt he remembered just how good. "I know Nana would be proud of you two."

Ruth was a strong woman who was dedicated to her husband and she worked tirelessly for her church. Ruth and Ray Hiebert always made Vince feel like he was their son, not just a son-in-law.

"Yes she'd be real proud." Melanie caught herself. "I miss shopping with Mom. She delighted in buying you two the cutest outfits. I still have most of them boxed up in the attic. I can't seem to let go of the memories of the times when you wore them."

Vince grabbed a water bottle from the console holder, twisted off the cap, and took a deep gulp. He peered at his wife. "Are you okay?"

"I'm fine," Melanie said. Her attempt at diversion was not difficult to see. "When do you think they will put the new carpeting in the family room? I hope they don't wait till the week before Christmas."

"No way." Vince wasn't really sure, but he understood diversions and it wasn't hard to figure out that Melanie missed her mom and it was best to talk about something else. "I'm sure they'll do it well before then."

Chapter 8

O ther school officials noticed Vince's success at Tecumseh. The superintendent of Dublin Schools did not just notice, he acted. Dublin's football program had the potential to win a state championship and their head football coach had just been named the principal at a new middle school in the district, which removed him from coaching. They offered Vince the head job, and although he loved his experience in New Carlisle, everyone associated with Tecumseh knew that this was an opportunity he could not refuse. After a wonderful going-away party thrown by Mike Weiland and the Boosters, the Sanfords packed up and headed to Dublin for Vince to face his next challenge.

The Sanfords lived in a condominium complex east of the Scioto River the first two years in Dublin. Condo life did not suit Vince, plus the children were growing. They all craved having their own place to call home, so purchasing a house moved to the top of the Sanford's priority list.

Vince had heard about a particular house from a friend and decided to approach the owner about placing a bid. The yard needed a lot of work and the interior would require some remodeling, but nothing major. The owner needed to sell quickly, which put Vince and Melanie in the perfect spot at the right time. The new home excited the entire family.

Melanie started her home makeover on the outside. She planted extra trees, a few bushes, and plenty of flowers. In the front yard, she placed an iron bench beneath the shade of an enormous oak tree. Vince suspected she did it to encourage them to sit down in the evening and watch the birds flying from tree to tree, as well as to let the neighbors see him without a whistle around his neck.

Inside their home, Melanie also worked her charm. The family gathering place was the dining area adjacent to the kitchen. The large room was decorated with a dark oak table big enough to easily seat six people but it worked best with four. Next to the window Melanie placed two comfortable wing chairs separated by a small coffee table. While she cooked dinner or completed lesson plans, the seating arrangement provided her excellent opportunities for scrutiny of her children's homework efforts.

After their family dinners, Vince took over by checking up on the kids' homework status and other sensitive areas like their group of friends. Vince wanted his children to know that he cared about them and who they were hanging around with at school. He loved to say, "You can't choose your relatives, but you can choose your friends."

During this check-up time, after Vince felt comfortable about homework and friends, he loved to share stories about the family— things his dad had done or how his mom could always bake the best sugar cookies or he could always come up with a good tale about Conrad or Lori. There was one exception: Vince got upset whenever he tried to figure out Frank. So, like his father, Vince chose to not talk about his grandpa.

Melanie closed her magazine and pulled down the visor to use the passenger mirror. Vince looked over and saw Melanie reaching into her purse. "Going to get pretty for the family, hey?" Vince teased.

"Just trying to look as beautiful as Taylor," Melanie smiled.

"Speaking of family," Vince turned the radio volume down. "Sean, you gonna sit in front of the TV today, or you think you might try to talk with some of your relatives?"

Sean did not get to answer. Taylor jumped in, "He already told me that he's watching the Detroit Lions." Her voice had that slight hint of tattling on her brother.

"Taylor," Sean scolded, "I can do both."

"You sure can, honey," Melanie said. "I think what your dad's suggesting is how important it is to spend time with family."

"Your mom's right. We don't get to see everyone as much as we like. It means a lot when you take some time to be with them. You know, getting to know each other better as you grow. Family is special."

"Mommy, who all is coming today?" Taylor asked. "Will Grandpa Frank be there?"

"No problem talking with him and watching the Lions," Sean said under his breath, but everyone in the car heard him and understood.

"Hey," Vince barked more at himself than at Sean. He had been thinking the same thing. "He's still your great grandpa."

"Your Uncle Conrad and Aunt Lori will be there with their families." Melanie turned slightly, keeping the conversation light.

Sean leaned towards Taylor giving his big brother stare. "I will be spending some time with family, Squirt. Jay and I will kick butt on anyone who tries to take us on in football."

"Bonnie and I will be in the basement, Creep." Taylor tossed the look back. "Hope you guys freeze."

Conrad was Vince's older brother who had just retired from the Air Force after twenty-seven years of distinguished service. He and his wife Jackie and Jay and Matt, their two sons, lived north of Ashland. Matt and Sean were about the same age. Jay was slightly older. When all the cousins were together there was no shortage of competition.

Lori was Vince's baby sister. Life had been very unfair to her, but you would not have known from any words that crossed her lips. After an ugly divorce, she and her only daughter Bonnie moved to Cincinnati where she worked as a nurse. Bonnie loved being with Taylor, who gleefully accepted the responsibility of teaching her younger cousin the fine art of dressing up like princesses or reading *Boston Jane* books.

"Don't forget. Peter got in yesterday," Vince added to the list. Peter was Vince's favorite cousin. He lived out in Ellensburg, Washington. He was a professor at Central Washington University and unfortunately only came back to Ohio on holidays. His wife, Barb, was a wonderful addition to the family. Peter Jr., their only child, was a year younger than Sean and an eager competitor in any Sanford family game.

"I can't wait to see Barb," Melanie sighed. "It has been over a year."

"It will be good to see Peter, too," Vince answered. Then he spoke to Sean. "Let me tell you something, boy. When Peter and I were your age we could have pounded you and your cousins in football. We would have scored so many touchdowns you would have needed an adding machine to tally them up."

"Dad, you won't mind if I ask Uncle Conrad for his recollection of how good you guys were?" Sean teased. "Was the forward pass legal when you guys played?"

"Nice one," Melanie rewarded her son's quick wit.

"Peter and I might just have to show you squirts that we still got it."

"Honey, this isn't *The Big Chill*," Melanie's voice was full of spirit. "You pull a muscle, don't expect to come crying to me."

The car echoed with laughter as Vince's thoughts shifted back to his dad. He enjoyed the teasing with Sean. It reminded him of the endless times Banner and he had mixed it up with friendly bantering. Banner had a robust wit about him and did not spare it on his children. Whether it be sports, education, or sweethearts, at the drop of a hat Banner could cause the family to erupt into laughter with a story or jovial harassment of a loved one.

Vince was the target on several occasions. He stared out at the highway ahead as he recalled Banner's version of his first skiing trip. *I should have known better. Why is it that the older and more mature we get that we realize that our parents were right all along. Why did I buck so much? I should have listened more.*

When Vince was in ninth grade, the Methodist Church youth group had planned a skiing trip. Although it was in the middle of basketball season, Vince begged to go.

"Basketball. You might need some sturdy legs for that sport." Banner advised. It was his first attempt at showing Vince that sometimes father knows best.

"Dad, everybody is going!" Vince pleaded.

"How many times have you been skiing?" Experience responded.

"Well, this would be my first time. But I know I can do it."

"Coach know you want to go skiing?" the voice of experience continued.

"He loves to ski."

"Does he **know** you want to go skiing?" Banner was persistent.

"Not exactly."

"What's 'not exactly' mean?'

"Well, I think he doesn't mind," Vince looked at his shoes.

"Banner why are you giving him a hard time?" Lorraine was focused on short term and had empathy for her son. "It's a church group. They're only going for a few hours."

"Dad, it will be only a few hours." Vince quietly thanked his mom with his eyes. He could see the ice melting on his dad's growl.

"Just remember I told you it's basketball season."

Banner loved to retell the beginning of the story. He then delighted in telling the rest of the story.

Banner would stare at Vince and smile. "The Olympic hopeful was enjoying the afternoon with his friends and all was well until the last run of the day. He had been using the beginning slopes and felt he was ready for the big time. As he was heading down the advance slope, disaster hit. There was a crash followed by a snap. It was the ankle."

The church group called from the hospital. The ride to Ashland Community Hospital only took a few minutes. The car remained silent the whole trip. Banner parked next to the emergency room and told Lorraine, "Let's go see what the x-rays show us."

The results were fast and damaging. The doctor confirmed the ankle was broken as he proceeded to prepare a cast.

"How many pairs of socks did you have on?" the doctor requested.

"I'm not sure, sir." Vince's face screamed that he was in pain but his inner toughness would not let one tear fall onto his cheek. "Maybe five. I didn't want my feet to freeze."

The doctor released some of the tension as his voice crackled with laughter. "That would normally do it. Your ankle had no give in it."

Vince hobbled on crutches back to the parked car. The ride home was just as quick. But it allowed time for Banner to drive home his point. "I tried my best. I think I said no at least three times." No response was needed and none was given.

The pain from a broken ankle was long gone as Vince drove his family to his parents for Thanksgiving, but the message lived on. *Bet I have to listen to that story again this weekend. Dad never complains. He has to be in pain from the treatments.*

Chapter 9

Vince rested his hand on the console. "Mom said Dad has handled the treatments as well as could be expected," Vince murmured.

Melanie reached over and gave his hand a warm, loving squeeze. "I know. I talked to Lori last Saturday. She said he has lost a lot of weight... and you know about his hair." Her words had turned into a whisper.

Sean had overheard. "Will Grandad be all right?"

"Grandad is pretty sick," Melanie offered.

"Hey, you know Grandad. He is a tough dude." Vince tried to reassure himself as much as his family. "It's just," he paused... "it's just this is a little different situation."

The whole family had been caught off guard with the news. Cancer. They were no stranger to the viciousness of the disease. A few friends, several people at church, and national exposure for the illness had made sure of that. *But Banner.* The man did not deserve this fate. He had traveled his life path with good intentions. He had smoked little, drank little, and always tried to watch his weight, although he could hold his own with anyone at the dinner table. It just did not seem fair.

"What should we do?" Sean was clearly concerned. "I mean, can I talk to Grandad?" His questions showed that he had been raised by a family who cared about each other. He had been exposed to a grandfather who, by simply living a good life, passed on lessons not only to his children, but also to his grandchildren. Through the years, Banner had set a good example on several occasions. When the grandchildren visited, he would lovingly focus on them rather than on TV or some other personal activity. He loved to take them to the Ashland library where they would look at hundreds of books and spend a few minutes on the computers. He would take them golfing when possible, and he never missed the opportunities to shoot a few hoops.

"Absolutely. You can still talk with Grandad," Melanie said, attempting to sound cheerful.

"How about basketball? You think Grandad will still want to shoot some?"

Banner had installed a hoop in the driveway for his kids early on. It had survived the summer heat and the harshest winters. It remained a sturdy target for all the grandchildren. Games of Pig, Horse, and Around the World had replaced the fierce two-on-two games of Vince's youth, but the degree of competition had not diminished. Banner and Vince had each been decent shooters. However, as time passed and both grew older, Sean had passed them by in skill. Around the World was entertaining, but Sean's accuracy was overpowering. The older guys would try to hang in as long as possible before the inevitable would happen.

"We will have to wait and see on that one," Vince said. "Sean, I sure would love if he could."

Vince privately switched his thoughts to more practical matters. He was happy that his parents had paid off their mortgage and owned their house outright. Even Banner's Plymouth van had no monthly payments. "I sure am glad that Dad had good medical benefits through F.E. Myers," Vince said, expecting that Melanie would be the only one who heard the statement. He was wrong.

Taylor had been listening quite intently for the last few miles. "Dad, what exactly are medical benefits?"

Before answering, Vince looked out his side window. Cornfields that had been harvested weeks earlier stared back at him. "Honey, it basically means you have a lot of help paying your doctor bills when you get sick."

Melanie turned slightly in the passenger's seat. "Vince, you probably need to talk with your Mom to make sure their coverage is still okay."

Vince had assumed that his dad's coverage was good, but he really did not know. "You are probably right," He sheltered the concern in his voice. "With Conrad and Lori there, it will be a good time to check to make sure."

The big green and white interstate sign announced that Mansfield was the next exit. Vince knew they were getting close. The Ashland exit was only a few miles beyond Mansfield. Vince addressed the passengers. "Hey guys, thanks for letting me ramble on a little bit. I don't know if any of the stuff we have talked about will stick, but I sure hope so."

Chapter 10

Vince released the cruise control. He steered the Jeep onto the exit and weaved down to the stop sign. Ashland to the left; Wooster to the right. He had been at this Route 250 intersection thousands of times. The demands of coaching and teaching had limited the times in recent years, but had not diminished the good feeling created by making the left turn and heading into his old town.

The Rt. 250 truck stop was still there and so was the small motel on the north side of the road. The sun broke free from the clouds long enough to heighten Vince's warm feelings. He was headed home. The familiar restaurant farther down the road seemed to be saying to him, "Good to see you again, Vince." Even the old carwash looked good to his eyes. It seemed to offer its own greeting. "Hey man, where you been?"

As they passed the bowling alley, Sean asked, "Dad, you ever bowl in there?"

"A few times. I wasn't very good at bowling. And besides, it cost money to play that game," Vince smiled. "I had to play the free sports when I was growing up."

"Your Aunt Lori is a pretty good bowler," Melanie contradicted. "I guess she must have had a scholarship." Sean and Taylor laughed at their mother's jab.

Vince ignored the poke. "That's where I went to kindergarten." He nodded towards an elementary school. His family had heard him make that statement just about every time they passed the site. It was an old two-story brick building that held more fond memories for him. His teacher, Mrs. Starling, an older, refined woman, was strong in heart and even stronger in compassion. Each day started with the class lined up outside her door. As students entered, they were greeted with a hug that warmed the hearts of the children like a cozy fire on a cold winter's night.

Mrs. Starling would have made anyone's all-star team on stressing the difference between right and wrong. Along with everyone else, Vince learned that it was best to say "Yes Ma'am or No Sir." Sharing was the right thing to do and cleaning up after yourself was expected. Vince could hear her words today: "Treat others like you want to be treated, children."

She was proud to lead her class in the Pledge of Allegiance and understood its importance. Being a devout Baptist did not prevent her from being tolerant of all religions. She stood up for her faith, as well as others, and completely understood the power of setting a good example. Vince and his classmates observed their teacher every morning sitting at her desk, quietly saying a personal prayer before the first lesson.

"Mrs. Starling was the best." Vince cleared his throat, choked up with the memories.

"Dad, did you go to first grade there, too?" Taylor asked.

"No, I went to elementary school on the other side of town." Vince answered. "Teachers had to work at it, but they finally got me to read and write." Vince chuckled. His family had come to love that sound.

"Dodge ball!" Vince declared. "One of the things I remember most about school was dodge ball. I loved dodge ball."

"Why does that not surprise me?" Melanie grinned.

"It was great. The teacher would split us up. Half on one side of the gym floor and half on the other. We would line up against the back walls and when the whistle blew we would sprint to midcourt, grab the balls, and start firing at each other." Vince shook his head. "Boy, did we pound some kids."

Vince could see that the next light was turning red so he pulled to a slow stop. "Mrs. Hurd, my second grade teacher. She's the one who first introduced me to Narnia."

Taylor gasped. "I love *The Lion, the Witch, and the Wardrobe*."

"We all did, too," Vince tilted his head to the rear. "Mrs. Hurd would take us for a walk down by a creek back behind the school, saying she was taking us into Narnia. She would read page after page to our class."

Vince let himself recapture the smell of the oak trees that bordered the creek. In the fall, their brown and orange leaves would blanket the ground around the rock where Mrs. Hurd always sat with her flock of students scattered all around her. Discipline was not a problem in her class. Each child listened with the earnestness of deer taking a sip along the creek while watching for an intruder. Often the sun would shine down through the outstretched limbs and sparkle on the faces enthralled with what might happen in the magical world of Narnia.

"I think Mrs. Hurd really made a difference in encouraging me to read." Vince stepped on the gas pedal and drove through the intersection. "Guess this is the first time I ever realized that."

"Well, well, well." Melanie brightened her smile. "The big guy finally understands that we elementary teachers have a few tricks up our sleeves, too."

The Jeep kept moving down route 250 right into the heart of downtown Ashland. This town showed the signs of what small town America used to look like before the Wal-Marts, car dealerships, and fast food chains dictated where people would shop and have dinner.

Many establishments and stores still operated, but they did not thrive like they had in the 1950s and 1960s. The bank was still there on the corner, however. Its name had changed three times and it had seen many neighbors come and go over the last fifty years.

A gas station stood right on the edge of downtown, just before the stores started filling the street. Through the years, the Sanfords had been regular customers at that station. Early on, along with his tank of gas, Banner would purchase a Nehi orange soda and a Moon Pie when he was out on errands. When Vince started driving, he loved to stop after practice and chug an ice cold Pepsi before heading home. Doug, the owner, had always offered to clean Banner's windshield, but by the time Vince was behind the wheel, no such customer care service existed.

"Wonder what ever happened to Doug? He's the guy who used to own that station. Dad always liked him."

No Main Street in America would be complete without a few bars. Ashland had its share. The most popular was an establishment call Third Base. Its slogan was "If you are heading home, you should hit third first!" The main bartender had played football for the Ashland Arrows back in the early 70s and had a great personality. He was friendly with his pours and always had a good ear. Through the years even Third Base had changed. In Banner's younger days, customers would order a Carlings Black Label beer and did not have a clue what lite meant, unless someone was referring to getting something to fire up their cigarette. Background music moved from primarily rock and roll to mostly country, especially Alan Jackson, Kenny Chesney, and Faith Hill.

The bar food was pretty limited, but if someone liked hamburgers or hot dogs it was just right. Banner had played softball when he was a young adult. His team, the River Rats, had regularly filled up one corner after their games.

As he was growing up, Vince had visited the Third Base often. One memorable visit was during the ninth grade when Banner took the family there for a good hamburger one Friday night.

Banner found a table in the back room, where the noise coming from the tables made it pretty clear that it was the beginning of the weekend and the customers wanted to let off some steam. The far wall was plastered with pennants from all the Big Ten schools and most of the Mid-American Conference. Pictures of former athletic greats were scattered about on every wall. Vince was familiar with most of them because Banner had provided detailed explanations for each. "Now that one is the great Jimmy Brown. He played for the Browns back in the 60s". Banner shook his head. "Still hasn't been one better." He then pointed at the picture above it. "Ernie Davis. Ernie Davis. I bet there aren't two guys in here who know that's Ernie Davis." Banner took a sip of his drink. "Man never got to play with the Browns. Was an All-American at Syracuse just like Jimmy Brown, but he got ill. Some type of leukemia or something." Banner took another sip. "Lord must have thought it would be unfair to have those two guys running in the same backfield." Vince could understand from his dad's voice that they had to be really great, but his own appreciation of a good running back was still Marcus Allen or Emmitt Smith.

"Now look at that guy." Banner gazed at the baseball pictures. "Rocky Colovito. He was one powerful batter. Could jack any pitcher. He would demoralize some of the young guys on the mound today."

Banner pointed at the east wall. "Dave Crecelius." He shook his finger for emphasis. "This picture was taken from the 1982 Holiday Bowl. Dave was from outside of Ashland and was a defensive lineman." Banner's voice deepened. "The picture you're looking at was when the Buckeyes were playing BYU. Who was the left-handed QB they had?"

"Steve Young." Vince liked answering the question even though he had heard the story a dozen times.

"Yeah that's right." Banner would stop to get eye contact with everyone at the table. "Well that pretty boy had a bad day and his worst moment was when Crecelius drilled him from the back side. I think it was in the third quarter. The next thing Steve knew, it was 1983!"

Vince stopped for a moment, rubbed his hand through his hair. He looked through the windshield and pictured his dad back in those days. Sturdy, firm of voice, full of wit, and a joy to be around. *Dang Cancer! I hope Dad is able to get out of bed today.*

He went back to his recollection of that Friday night at the Third Base. The waitress had just delivered everyone's meals when Vince saw his Dad lean over to Lorraine and say, "Honey, do you see what is going on over at that table?"

The table he asked about was filled with two local mothers sitting with their sons and young dates. Three pitchers of beer were spread out across the table, along with six clear plastic cups filled with beer.

"Vince, you know those girls over there?" Banner asked quietly.

"Sure Dad. They're juniors at Ashland High School. Why?"

Banner did not answer. He looked at Lorraine. "No way they're old enough to be drinking in here," said Banner.

The waitress came back to check on the Sanford's food. Banner rubbed his bottom lip, then in a soft voice asked, "Can you come over here for a minute?" The waitress looked like she was prepared to help correct someone's poorly cooked meal, Banner surprised her. "Is a manager here tonight? I'm sure that he would appreciate knowing that over at that table at least two of those kids are not old enough to be drinking."

The waitress had waited on the table in question, but she looked on the scene with new eyes. She whispered, "Thank you. I'll get John. He's the manager." She lifted her tray and scurried to the other side of the restaurant.

Soon John, a stocky guy with thinning hair combed straight back, went over to the table and seemed to be forcefully addressing Banner's concern.

One mother stood up in a huff and growled at John, "Fine! We are leaving!"

The other mom headed straight to the Sanfords' table and spoke straight at Banner. "Who do you think you are? The manager said you complained about us. Can't you mind your own business?"

Vince watched his Dad's eyes focus, his jaw stiffen. Lorraine was too late. She tried to grab Banner's arm, but he was up and in the mother's face. "You want to question me? My motives? What actually inspires a mother to let her children drink alcohol when she knows full well it is illegal and wrong? And these young girls aren't even yours!"

Vince was sure that the mother could see the steam coming from his dad and felt the daggers from his stare. Then she made her best decision of the evening. Throwing her hair back, she exhaled a pitiful, "Well!" She turned quickly to catch up to the rest of her group as they were headed out the door.

As Banner put the mother in her place, Lorraine went over to the two young girls and offered to give them a ride home. The girls sheepishly said, "No thank you, Ma'am," and walked out with the group. Banner and Lorraine sat back down with their family.

"There is a time and a place for everything." Banner preached. "Alcohol is not always bad. It is the way people misuse it, like the girls at that table, or let it control their lives that creates problems. I truly am sorry that you all had to watch that happen." Banner took a deep breath, and patted Lorraine's arm for her efforts. "But I hope it has been a valuable lesson."

Chapter 11

Vince looked past the next intersection. The Ashland Cemetery stretched out for acres. He had been there several times— none of them happy. He had mourned the passing of his grandparents from his mother's side of the family. He tried to picture their faces, but his recollection was not powerful enough. He was only eight when they both died. He was told the story many times about how his Grandmother Rose barely outlived his grandfather. It turned out his Grandfather Harry was so saddened by Rose's being in the hospital for a heart problem, he had a stroke and never recovered. Rose passed away six months later. It was not a good year for the family. Lorraine had tried to make sense of her loss. "Mom and Dad had good lives. They created a loving family, and both are now at peace with the Lord."

Driving past the cemetery, Vince had a sudden chill. *Dad's sick, but what if Mom's having a problem handling this?* He slowed the Jeep just a little and looked over at Melanie. "You suppose Mom's doing okay? You know with Dad's situation? Do you think she is handling things all right?'

Melanie cleared her throat. "Vince, she is a tough lady. You know that. Maybe you should ask Conrad and Lori."

"I will," Vince sighed. "It's just with Dad the way he is, it's real difficult. But Mom could be hurting big time and we don't even know it." Vince put both hands on the steering wheel. "I can't stop thinking about what happened to Harry and Rose."

"Honey, be thankful that you have a chance to be with your parents, to check things out." Melanie's voice reminded him how thankful he was to have found such a precious woman to share his life.

Changing the topic of conversation, Vince turned his attention to the back seat, "So Sean, you guys figure out who's playing who in the big football game today? And I don't mean the Detroit Lions."

"Teams are already set," Sean said with authority. "Matt and I are taking on Peter and Jay. We will pound them."

"I'm sure you will. I'm sure you will." Vince felt a bit of relief as Sean's words brought a little light heartedness back into the car.

Vince had to slow down as a car stopped in front of them to make a left-hand turn into Tag's Market, a small neighborhood grocery store. "Look at that place. After all these years it is still surviving." Vince commented about the store's full parking lot. "With all the big supermarkets and Wal-Mart as competition, Tag's just keeps on ticking."

"Taylor," Vince hesitated. "I can remember going in there when I was in first grade. Loved to get a Pepsi and Milky Way." Vince's smile felt good on his face. "Your Grandma would send me and your Uncle Conrad up there for bread and milk or some other things she said she had to have immediately or dinner would be a mess."

The car turned and Vince stepped on the accelerator. "Now I have to drink Diet Pepsi and I can only dream about eating a candy bar!"

Vince finally turned on his blinker to make the turn on to Sharon Avenue. Two houses down on the left side sat his parents' home. No matter how many places he would live in his life, this one would always be home. Banner and Lorraine had made it so. This is where family values were set in motion The Sanfords fostered an atmosphere for forgiveness, compassion, and respect for others and they ensured their three children adhered to these values. Church was important, and honoring the Sabbath even more so. Vince and his siblings had received the constructive discipline that led to the development of good character and were taught that being truthful and honest are not always easy, but they are always the right paths to follow.

Over two decades later, those memories and those teachings were in Vince's heart as he pulled into the driveway. He wanted to jump out of the car, hug his mom, and let his hug express the love and concern he had for her. His arms would shout: *You are safe. Don't worry.*

He wanted to look his dad in the eye, shake his hand, then pull him close for a hug. The firmness of his grip and the clearness in his eye would let his dad know that after all these years, he gets it. *Your work with your kids was worth it, Dad. I get it.*

Chapter 12

Parked in front of the closed garage door was a gray Mercury. "Matt and Jay are here," Sean hollered. "That's Uncle Conrad's car."

The side door swung open allowing two young men who were true reflections of their father to pounce towards the Jeep. Built like young prizefighters, their eyes sparkled as they approached the Sanfords.

Sean popped his door open and rushed to get out. "Matt, what's happening?" They shook hands enthusiastically.

"Where you been, man? We've been waitin' an hour," Jay snorted as Sean high five-ed his older cousin.

"Sorry boys," Melanie stepped out of the passenger's seat. "Our chauffeur took the scenic route." Melanie held out her arms to them. "Look at the size of you guys. I swear you're both as big as your dad." Melanie hugged them both. As Matt pulled away he noticed Taylor standing with her arms folded, waiting for attention.

"Hi Taylor."

"Hi guys," she grinned.

"Dad, is the back unlocked?" Sean was reaching for the handle. "I want to show them the new Rawlings."

"Should be." Vince slid out and walked to the back of the Jeep to start unloading their bags. "What's going on guys?"

"Hi Uncle Vince." The cousins sounded like a choir. Jay patted Vince's back. "Mom and Dad are sure looking forward to seeing you. Dad said he's gonna' whip you in Rook tonight."

"Don't think so!" Vince sat a bag down on the driveway. "It's your Aunt Lori he's got a shot at beating."

"Aunt Lori called Grandma about two hours ago. Said they were on their way," Matt answered. "Should be here pretty soon."

"Yeah, she called Dad, too, as we were leaving Dublin," Sean added.

"I called Peter ten minutes ago. They were just about to leave Haysville." Jay followed Sean to the back of the Jeep. "They'll be here in no time."

"That means we'll be stompin' you guys before noon," Matt boasted, roughly pushing Jay out of his way.

Sean grabbed the new Rawlings from the back of the Jeep. "Check this baby out," he boasted, tossing the ball to Matt.

"Give me that," Jay's quick hands stripped the ball from Matt. He darted towards the back yard. The other two raced after him.

"I don't think so, boys," Melanie yelled after them. "Sean and Taylor have to say hi to the rest of the family before any games get fired up."

"Sorry, boys. Nothing I can do for you. Your Aunt Melanie is right." Vince understood their need to play. "Taylor, you grab that suitcase. Sean, help me with these pies."

Jay ran back to the Jeep reluctantly, but composed himself quickly. "Matt, let's get that stuff for Uncle Vince," Jay said with forced maturity in his voice. "You all will want to see Grandad right away."

Jay's words shot through Vince, an arrow piercing unprotected flesh. He had not seen his father for over a month. They opened the side door to the house and Taylor was first to enter. "Grandma!" she shouted as she swept across the kitchen floor to steal the first hug.

Mom looks tired. He tried to dismiss the thought. *She always works herself into a frenzy before any family gathering.* Lorraine was a short, hearty woman whose face bestowed kindness to every visitor. Her hazel eyes sparkled with pure delight when they gazed at family. Her once black hair was now covered with grey and cut short to let the curls do, as she described, "what they will." Her favorite apron was wrapped around her green checkered dress the family had seen her wear dozens of times, a knee-length lavender canvas with "Grandma's Kitchen" stitched across the front.

"Well, it is good to see everyone." Love swelled from Lorraine's voice.

Sean waited for his hug next. Melanie's followed. Vince was grabbing his mom when he heard the deep voice of his brother through the hallway.

"About time you got here," Conrad spouted with an air of gladness. "The boys have been biting at the bit for that kid of yours to show up." Conrad winked at his nephew then playfully rubbed his hand across Sean's crew cut as he walked by. "But, this is the one I have been waiting for," Conrad lifted Taylor off her feet and swirled her around. "How is the Princess of Dublin?"

Taylor giggled as her toes touched back down to the floor.

Frank sat silently at the end of the kitchen table. He gave them a bland smile of acknowledgement, but said nothing. Vince reached over and squeezed his shoulder. "Good to see you, Grandpa."

Lorraine slipped both arms around Vince's waist and squeezed tenderly. "He's been feeling really well lately. Haven't you, Frank?" Frank shook his head slightly without looking up.

Turning his mom towards him, Vince hesitated before asking the question he had been asking himself the whole ride. "How is Dad?" Vince knew his mom heard the unexpected quiver in his voice.

Lorraine squeezed her son's hand. "Come with me. He has been so anxious to see you."

"Vince, you go ahead." Melanie appeared to notice Lorraine had not specifically answered Vince. "The rest of us will talk with Jackie and Conrad for a while. You go see Dad first."

Vince expected a typical sly remark by Conrad to make everyone laugh and lighten the sudden tense feeling in the room. None was given.

Vince released his Mom's hand and followed her down the hallway into the living room towards the stairs. Passing through the living room, there was the ancient green sofa where he had sat with his dad watching any sports coverage they could find on lazy Sunday afternoons. Its arms were worn thin and the cushions sagged in the middle. The sofa had aged, but Lorraine was not about to replace it. Memories were too precious.

Lorraine moved carefully up the stairs. Arthritis in her knees was evidently worse. She limped slowly, one step at a time. She stopped at the top and turned slightly as if to apologize for her shortness of breath. Vince responded, "I'm right behind you. You okay, Mom?" His voice was anxious.

"I'd be fine without these steps." Lorraine brightened as she crossed the doorway of the master bedroom, calling happily, "Banner, look what just got in from Dublin."

Vince watched his father try to sit up in bed but slowly lie back as if the effort was just too great. He forced a jovial smile as he walked towards the side of the bed and sat down on the empty side.

Banner had been a sturdy man all his adult life. His barrel chest and strong forearms were formed from the hard labor throughout his life. The man Vince now saw was only a shadow of the man who had made Vince run before he could take a dip in the Brookside pool. The man Vince was looking at now could not have weighed 150 pounds and his skin was white as the snow Vince had been driving through for the past few hours.

Chapter 13

"**G**ood to see you, son." Banner's soft voice seemed to understand his son's pain. "Look at your mother. She sure is beautiful today, isn't she?"

"She's beautiful any day," was Vince's quick response. Lorraine tilted her head accepting without comment the compliment from two of her men. "Dad, you on that South Beach Diet? I think you've lost some weight." Vince tried to joke, but he regretted his words as soon as they escaped his mouth.

Both Banner and Lorraine burst out with laughter. Each seemed to relish the escape from pain for the moment. Banner gripped his son's hand. "No, son, I'm not on some diet. It's all those bland vegetables your mom is making me eat now." Banner fidgeted slightly "Boy, would I like a big steak." Banner closed his eyes and moved his lips as if tasting a juicy rib eye.

"Dad, sorry I can't accommodate that wish. We'd both be on mom's bad boy list." Vince squeezed his father's hand as he continued. "Have the doctors said any more?" There was no more forced jovialness in Vince's words. He was aching and needed to hear something good.

"You know the doctors. They say I have to keep taking the treatments and see what happens." Banner's words did not deliver the message Vince wanted to hear.

"Honey, the good news is," Lorraine spoke then hesitated, "the good news is that the doctors still feel that there is a chance that increasing the dosage might be the answer."

"Can you walk, or...?" Vince did not get to finish his question.

"Yes, I can get around fine, but the warden over there," Banner winked at Lorraine, "she says I have to limit myself."

"I'm just doing what the doctors say to, darling. Vince, you know your dad," she said, with a hint of "Help me" in her voice.

"Dad, Mom is probably right."

Banner frowned, letting them know what he thought about limitations.

"Once Lori and Bonnie get here, we'll help you down and the family will have a wonderful dinner," Lorraine pleaded.

"That's not like Lori. She should have been here already. She's usually first to arrive at any gathering," Banner sounded worried.

"There was a lot of traffic, Dad." Vince tried to fluff up the pillow behind Banner to make him more comfortable. "I'm sure they will be here in a little while."

Vince peered around the room. There was the dark red chest of drawers Vince remembered from his childhood. The same white rotary dial Ohio Bell phone sat on the night stand along with an alarm clock that had survived at least two decades. On the far wall was Lorraine's small chest of drawers that held family pictures from each of her three children. On the wall above the dresser was a large mirror which made the room seem bigger. Next to the mirror was a picture of the Haysville home Lorraine had lived in as a child.

"Vince, you stay with your dad. I have to get back to my kitchen or something will burn."

"Sure," Vince said absently. "Hey, Mom? Ask Melanie to bring the kids up. Okay?"

Lorraine kissed the top of Vince's head as she walked by the bed. "I'll send them right up."

Chapter 14

G lancing back towards his dad, Vince saw an abundance of wrinkles he had never noticed before. He saw hands that could not hold a hammer or firmly squeeze pruning shears as they had so effortlessly done in the past. "Dad, have you been able to sleep all right?" Before Banner could answer, Vince heard footsteps coming up the steps. "Just a second, I'll be right back."

Vince jumped off the bed and headed to the top of the stairs. He whispered while touching the arms of his two children. "Remember what I said on the drive up. Grandad is not feeling well and he has lost some weight. You just act like everything is fine, okay?"

"Sure Dad," Sean answered for his sister and himself.

Vince's chin tightened as he caught Melanie's sad glance. He forced a cheerful tone as they walked together into the room. "You've got some more fans wanting to see you, Dad."

"Hey Sean. Hey Taylor." Banner's eyes glowed with love. "How are my two best buddies from Dublin?"

"We're great Grandad," Taylor burst out with an answer then continued. "Sean was going to go play football, but Mom made him come in first."

Sean gave his sister an "I'll get you later" look. Banner answered quickly, "Sean, I would have done the same. Come here, both of you and give me a hug."

Melanie leaned over the side of the bed and gave Banner a tender hug and kiss. "Good to see you, Dad." She then sat by him, sharing the bed and holding his hand as if she were his little girl, ready to tell a secret.

Conversation was light as Sean and Taylor shared what they had been doing all fall and Vince made sure that there were no moments of silence by adding stories about the last football season.

"You two have just about talked Grandad out before Thanksgiving dinner. Come with me. We'll let your dad visit a little more," Melanie turned towards the door as Sean and Taylor followed.

The room was suddenly silent. A ray of sunlight softly spread itself across the cream colored carpet. Vince pulled the armchair from its place by the window over to the bed and reached out to touch Banner's arm.

"Dad, it's been on my mind how you always encouraged us to do the right things. You know what I mean?" His fingers lingered lovingly around his father's arm. "How did you always know what was right?"

"Vince, Vince, you could always make my day," Banner laughed an almost-hearty laugh. "Who really knows what is right? We just lived day to day."

"I don't believe that. I think back to all the discipline. You making us work hard. The values you believed in. That was no accident." Vince's voice displayed his determination that two hours in a Jeep with his family had evoked.

Banner placed both hands behind his head and eased back against his pillow. "Do you remember when I thought you should run track rather than play baseball?"

"How could I forget?" Vince's grin grew. "I might now be playing for the Cleveland Indians if it wasn't for track."

"Maybe so, but I knew that you loved football more than anything. And sorry, son, but you needed speed!" Banner's laugh was stronger. "Well, who is to say if it was right or wrong? I just know those folks in Dublin think they have a damn good football coach. The truth, Vince, is that your mother and I never knew. We just tried to do our best. Point you kids in the right direction. I guess we hoped the Lord would take care of the rest."

Vince leaned back as his father's voice deepened. "Right and wrong comes down to everyone's own moral compass." Banner tried to sit up. "How that moral compass is built is different with everyone. Character is forged through years of practice." Banner hesitated. "You fumble one time and you might have to start all over from the beginning."

"Trust me, Dad. I know what you mean there. I have made more than a few mistakes."

"You think I never made any mistakes?" Banner pulled his blanket up towards his chest. "Let me give you some advice there. Keep 'em to yourself."

Vince appeared puzzled. "What do you mean?"

"I mean you're not the same guy who made those mistakes. You survived. Your kids need to see the role model that you have become, not the fool you might have been before Melanie straightened you out." Banner laughed with genuine glee.

That laugh was a welcomed sound. It gave Vince the courage to pursue the questions he had been struggling with for years. "Dad, I'm not the same guy." He paused, then continued. "Nor is Frank." He rubbed his chin. "Why won't you talk about him? What happened?"

"It's not worth talking about. Only causes more pain." All laughter had subsided.

"Dad, I should know. He is my grandfather, after all."

Banner turned on his side. The powerful stare that had routinely gripped Vince as a youngster was glaring at him once again. Banner sighed. "Yes, you should know." Banner waited what seemed like forever to continue. "My dad wasn't always the way he is now. They tell me that he was a hard worker in his early days. He loved your Grandma."

"How can that be? Now he just sits on the couch. Says hardly anything. Dad, he doesn't even seem to realize who his grandkids are when they're sitting right next to him."

"Vince, listen. I'm not going to talk about this again. I have never told your brother or sister. This is stuff no one needs to talk about."

"Dad, I'll listen."

"You listen. Then forget I ever told you anything. And don't tell your mom that we talked about this." Vince nodded. "Frank couldn't handle the bottle. Drinking caused him to get lazy, to screw up. First it was other women, then I think it was a little gambling mixed in. He was going downhill fast."

"Dad, that still does not explain why he is so silent and uncaring these days."

"Nobody that I'm familiar with really knows the exact facts about the rest of the story. They just know the ending. Frank and his father, my grandfather Ralph, must have had a falling out because something happened. Your Grandpa Frank had us living on the family farm and he was running it as a business for Ralph. For awhile things must have been pretty sound financially. My aunt and uncles on that side of the family most likely felt they were in line for a hefty inheritance. But guess what? Frank screwed up. His wayward living and gambling caused Ralph to lose the farm as well as any savings. We had to move and ended up renting a place north of Ashland."

Banner sighed. "I was too young to know or remember much. Not long after, your great grandfather was found dead in his car. They say it was suicide. The car was found not more than a mile from where we were living."

"You have got to be kidding! That really happened?"

"You wonder why I don't want to talk about it. Why I have never talked about it? All I know is Frank never recovered. He did get a factory job in Ashland for several years, but his condition just worsened. He became so withdrawn that even the factory had to let him go. Your mom and I have been paying for his apartment and trying to watch out for him the best we can these past 10 to 15 years."

"Wow!" Vince was awestruck with news.

"His brothers and sisters won't speak to him. They blame him for their father's death."

"Dad," Vince's voice carried compassion. "What can I do?"

"Not much you can do, Vince. You can't undo the ringing of a bell." Banner tightened his jaw. "Frank's my dad, son. You don't get to pick your relatives. He's probably doing the best he can. Lord only knows." Banner reached over and placed his hand upon his son's and squeezed once. "Just take care of your family."

Vince hoped Banner could not see the redness in his eyes. He sniffled "When do you have to take some more medicine?"

"Not till tonight," Banner coughed and shifted his position in bed. "Church…Church is the foundation for a strong moral compass."

Vince leaned back in his chair. He could tell his dad thought he had said enough about Frank and would say no more. Vince accepted the change in conversation.

"I'm mighty happy that your grandma made sure we went to Sunday school, then church," Banner said. "You know, I was like you, probably. At the time, I would have enjoyed missing. Any excuse would have been okay by me. But, looking back, it made a difference."

"Dad, I liked going to church," Vince said, then apologized. "Well, not like going to a movie or something, but Pastor Lillibridge was terrific. He had a way of making even the kids enjoy his sermons." Vince moved the chair closer to the bed. "Are Pastor Lillibridge and his wife coming over for dinner today?" Vince asked.

"I reckon so. Nick and Joanne have not missed sharing Thanksgiving with us for several years. They're like family."

"You know, Dad, I regret missing church when I'm coaching and stuff. You and Mom did teach us right."

"There you go, again. Trying to apologize to me." Banner's tone carried the message that he was not looking for sympathy. "Hey, I'm not dying. Just got this sickness I have to knock the crap out of." Banner tapped the bed sheets. "You're not old enough. All you and your brother and sister saw was us attending Ashland Methodist regularly. Your mom and I had a few lapses." Banner grinned. "You think I never gave Jesus a few headaches?"

"I hear you. I just wanted you to know that Sean and Taylor have a regular spot in Sunday School. I may have drifted some, but whatever you and Mom did, my roots got planted deep."

Enough had been said. Vince felt he should lighten the conversation. "What've you been watching on TV? Did you see the Buckeyes game last week?" Vince knew mentioning the Bucks would liven the atmosphere in the room.

"Give me a break. You think a little cancer is going to prevent me from watching the number one team in the nation?"

Now it was Vince's turn to laugh. "Dumb question."

Chapter 15

There was a tap on the door. "What are you two doing?" Peter walked in without an invitation. None was needed. He was the son of Banner's sister Sarah and her husband Dusty who had lived south of Ashland in Haysville. Unfortunately, both Dusty and Sarah had passed away several years back and now Peter was carrying the flag for that part of the family.

Growing up, Vince and Peter had been best friends. Peter was older by a few years and no doubt the better athlete of the two. He had a large body frame and a mustache that made people ignore where hair was lacking on the rest of his head. He had Dusty's hands, big and powerful, and he could never hide the cheerful smile inherited from his jolly Mom. When he stood by his only child, Peter Jr., no one ever questioned that they were father and son. Barb was a saint. She taught handicapped children in Ellensburg and was loved by her students.

Peter Jr. and Sean, like their fathers, enjoyed each other's company and relished any family gatherings that allowed them to share stories or play ball. Similar to Sean, Peter Jr. had been molded by positive family values and it clearly showed in his actions and manners. Nonetheless, he and his cousin were a work in progress, clearly having a little Tom Sawyer-like shenanigans spill out every once in awhile.

Peter grinned, "I figured you two would be up here taking a nap!" Vince could have sworn he heard his aunt's laugh. "The coast is clear. I took out the garbage and the potatoes are all peeled."

Vince stood up and stretched. "I knew you were good for something."

"Hey, Peter!" Banner reached for Peter's hand and pulled him into a hug. "So everybody is getting ready, huh?" Banner coughed.

"Barb and Melanie are helping Aunt Lorraine in the kitchen. Vince, you know Taylor, she's in the basement playing dress-up and waiting for Bonnie," Peter reported.

Vince rubbed the side of his head. "I know where the boys are."

Peter shook his head in agreement. "Maybe we should go outside and show those punks how to really play some football."

"Now, Peter, why would you want to do that?" Banner asked with a pinch of sarcasm. "You want your cousin over there to have to drive back to Dublin with a pulled muscle?" Banner's bedroom was again filled with laughter.

"Uncle Banner, hope you're feeling better."

"The doctor says I have been one of his better patients. You think he just says that to all his patients?"

Right then came one of those moments of silence that everyone hates. Vince was not prepared to answer his dad, nor was Peter.

"I swear!" Banner smashed the silence. "Would you two stop acting like that?"

Banner wiped the bottom of his nose with his handkerchief. "I'm going to be fine."

"Sorry, Dad." He knew Banner did not need to be reminded every minute about his misfortune. "Do you need us to go downstairs so you can get some rest?" Peter nodded.

"What kind of lame excuse is that?" Banner turned his head. "You guys think I am a rookie? What time do the Lions play?" Banner sneaked a smile.

"Uncle Banner, they come on in a couple of minutes at noon," Peter said politely.

"Lorraine wanted to eat at about two, so maybe I should rest a little," Banner's voice was much softer. "Vince, why don't you come get me just before dinner?"

"Sure thing, Dad."

"Hey, Peter," Banner raised his voice softly. "Are Lori and Bonnie here yet?"

"Don't think so."

"Should have been here by now." Banner pulled at his sheets.

"Come on, Vince. Let's let this guy get some rest," Peter started for the door. "Uncle Banner, we'll let you know as soon as Lori pulls into the driveway."

Downstairs the house was glowing. The kitchen was lively with conversation and the smells left no doubt it was Thanksgiving Day. Vince and Peter stepped into the kitchen to offer their assistance and to sneak a sample of Lorraine's deviled eggs.

"Anything we can do?" Peter made a weak offer.

"I believe everything's under control." Lorraine answered. "We're just making the salad and keeping an eye on the turkey."

"Smells good in here. Let me know if you need an official taste tester to make sure the food is safe for our family," Vince said, smiling over at his mom.

Melanie knew her husband too well. "You just keep your hands where we can see 'em and wait patiently, just like everyone else."

Defeated, Vince took a deep breath as he sat down at the table by Frank. Unlike any time before in his life, he reached over to his Grandpa and rubbed his arm. "These girls doing a good job, Grandpa?" Frank still did not say anything, just gave his usually nod. That did not seem to bother Vince any more. *What has this man gone through?*

Vince looked deeply into Frank's eyes. He tried to convey with his eyes to his grandfather that he wished he had known. Wished he had known what tragedies had been heaped on his plate. Maybe he could have been a better grandson. Vince wished that he could erase countless years of uncomfortable feelings. *Dad's right. You can't un-ring a bell. But I sure can start acting like a grandson.* He reached back over and embraced Frank's hand, giving it a gentle squeeze. "Grandpa, tell you what. This Thanksgiving dinner I'm sitting by you. I think that's the best seat in the house."

Frank slowly met his grandson's loving gaze. Vince felt a slight squeeze on his hand. *Were those tears?*

Frank's response, the warm kitchen and succulent smells wafting from the oven helped Vince feel content. He squeezed Frank's hand one more time and then looked over at the counter, previewing the desserts he would have the privilege of doing some damage to after dinner. His favorite was the pumpkin pie. Put a big scoop of vanilla ice cream on top and life was good. He was no stranger to the family recipe cherry cheese cake Barb had bought. He mentally calculated if he would have space for a piece of that and the lemon pie he spied next to the cookie jar filled with his mother's sugar cookies. On this day, there were no rules. All those diet gurus would be tied up out back with the dogs. Tomorrow he would listen to them bark about what he should or should not eat.

"Is Dad resting?" Melanie asked.

"Yes." Vince answered. "He was worried about Lori. She didn't call, did she?"

"Nobody's called," Barb offered.

"You know your sister. She is just probably running late," Lorraine answered. Her voice did a poor job of covering her concern.

Vince thought to himself, *I used almost those exact words just a few minutes ago. Amazing.* "You're right, Mom. That's my sister. She better have that special cheese ball or I'm sending her back to Cincinnati. Bonnie can stay, but she's going back."

The room gradually filled with animated conversation, each person seeming to jump in the best they could, holding their private thoughts about the day, their life, Banner, and concerns for Lori while they waited for their next opportunity to say something. Barb shared some experiences she had just had with her students and Peter bragged about how good the Central Washington basketball team would be this year.

Vince poured himself a cup of coffee at the counter and peered out the window. The mug sparkled. When Lorraine went on a cleaning quest she had a way of making sure that not only were the windows clean, but the whole house down to the dishware was shining. Each room was spotless and colorfully decorated for the season to perfection. Arthritis may have slowed her down, but it obviously had not defeated her.

Glancing out the window, Vince watched the Thanksgiving Day football game being played in Banner's backyard. Matt and Sean were leaning against each other and Matt had both his hands perched upon Sean's shoulders. *This should be interesting,* Vince smiled to himself as he watched Matt's lips moving at a rapid pace, undoubtedly calling a sure touchdown play. Jay and Peter Jr. were dug in, ready for the ball to be snapped. They were only about fifteen feet from the garden hose being used as a goal line.

The two offensive players clapped their hands as if they were breaking the huddle for the Pittsburgh Steelers. Jay and Peter Jr. dug in deeper. Sean snapped the ball to his cousin. After a fake to the inside, Sean headed to the corner with Peter Jr. on his tail. Jay was a relative, but that did not stop him from gathering speed to propel himself into Matt, who had just seconds to spare before releasing the football. It was a perfect pass heading right for Sean's raised hands. As his two thumbs were touching and preparing to secure the ball, Peter Jr.'s right hand pulled Sean's arm straight to his side. The ball fell to the ground. Incomplete pass.

Matt was lying on his back, recovering from the blow from his brother as Sean slid belly-first into the end zone. Jay and Peter Jr. popped up like bread out of a toaster and were headed to each other, prepared to exchange high fives.

Vince said nothing, letting his memories envelop him for a few minutes. He recalled how he loved to play the same game against Peter, Conrad, and the Miller boy who lived on the next block. Those were rough games, yet amazingly, no one ever really got hurt. A few bumps and bruises, maybe, but no bones broken. Winning was important back then, but now Vince could not even remember who won most often. He just remembered the joy of catching a pass or the thrill of an open field tackle, and the friendly bond that took place when you looked into the eyes of a teammate after a big play.

Vince watched Jay and Peter Jr. preparing to go on offense when thoughts of Lori resurfaced. He turned to his mom. "Hey, why don't we try to reach Lori on her cell phone?"

"I'd like that," Lorraine answered softly. "It's just not like Lori to be late for a family gathering. She's usually first to come and help me."

"Vince, you go ahead and call," Melanie suggested.

"Sure."

After punching in the numbers, Vince ran his right hand through his hair.

Peter could not resist an opportunity to heckle his cousin, "Better not do that too much or the rest will fall out, old man."

Vince did not need to answer. Everyone in the kitchen chuckled as he listened to the phone's ringing. He continued to listen while nodding in acceptance of Peter's attempt at humor. After several rings, Vince placed the phone back in the cradle. "Nothing, no answer."

"Why didn't you leave a message?" Conrad asked.

"Should have. I will next time. I'll try to call again in a few minutes."

"I'm sure they are all right," Lorraine spoke, but her voice carried a clear message that she was troubled by her daughter's absence. "You little guys clear out of here. We know the game is about to come on and we still have some work to do for dinner."

"Now that's a caring mom! Vince did I every tell you how much I love our mom?" Conrad gave Lorraine a peck on the cheek.

"I believe you have, I believe you have," Vince gave his brother a squeeze on the shoulder as they headed for the living room to watch the game. "Come on, Grandpa. Why don't you come with us?" Frank looked up at Vince's request, silently stood, and then followed the group to the other room.

Chapter 16

P eter sat in the sofa chair that was a prized seat for watching games because it was accompanied by an ottoman footstool. Vince grabbed the brown leather recliner that was Banner's favorite. Conrad guided Frank to the couch. "Right here, Frank. You can share the couch with me."

The front window looked right out onto Sharon Avenue. The neighbors across the street had a beautiful two-story home with hunter green shutters. Vince admired their newly painted cranberry red door set off with a golden kick plate. The lone tree in the front lawn was a tall maple that had survived the climbing of at least two generations of youngsters trying to prove their courage.

Conrad started to flip through the channels to locate the game. "Why do they put some of this junk on TV anyway?" His voice could not hide his disgust.

Peter was quick to respond. "I think they just like to aggravate you."

"Yeah, what ever happened to the good stuff we watched?" Vince added.

"You must mean something like *Rockford Files* or *Miami Vice*." Peter grinned.

"Now wait a minute," Conrad said. "Those shows had some violence, but they were family shows!"

"Yeah, right," said Peter. "You ever watch a rerun of *Miami Vice?* I believe there were a few babes dancing to the music." Peter leaned back in the sofa. "Our parents did not like what we watched. We don't like what our kids watch. It is as simple as that."

"So what's the answer?" Conrad asked.

Vince took a deep breath. His emotions were churning. Life seemed so fragile. *Dad's sickness. Frank's story. Why had Lori not called? Mom trying to hide her pain.* In an effort to calm his feelings, he answered his brother's question, "Could be we just have to keep working with our kids. Talking to them. Helping them recognize that life holds choices, decisions, consequences."

"Hey, lighten up, dude. It's Thanksgiving." Peter looked at him with a worried expression.

Vince realized how heavy his words must have sounded. They had no clue what he had been brewing over since he pulled out of his garage early this morning. "Sorry guys," he hesitated. "I mean, Conrad, Dad didn't just let us watch TV whenever we wanted to. He was one of the last on the block to order ESPN."

"God bless ESPN or we would still be waiting for Dad to have cable in this house." Conrad chuckled and sat up on the couch. "Tell you what, the more I think about it, that son of a gun rarely let us sit in front of the tube."

"I know, I know." Vince nodded. "We had to do our homework or something else around the house."

"Like cutting the grass," Conrad said the words in such a way the agony of the chore still seemed with him. "And then we were always involved with something at school."

"What about that singing thing you did?" Peter asked Vince with an expression meant more as a tease. "Hey, Frank. Did you know that Vince could sing?" Frank made no attempt to answer. Nothing had changed his behavior.

"What singing thing?" Vince answered leaving Frank with his private thoughts. "You mean Shalalee?"

"Yeah, isn't that the one you did just to sing and dance with the babes?" Conrad quizzed.

"You guys should hear me sing in church. I'm still pretty good," Vince pushed the leg rest down on the recliner and looked over at Peter. "Right and wrong. We have to help our kids with right and wrong." He leaned forward. "Conrad," he turned facing his brother. "It's simple. Got to pass on the values that Mom and Dad tried to give us. Problem is, when do you know if you are?"

"Let me give you a clue, Vince. You are," Peter's voice was now serious. "I know I have tried to with young Peter."

"That's kind." Vince tried to respond.

"No, let me finish. Have you watched your children?"

Vince again tried to reply, but Peter held his hand up like a traffic cop and then continued. "You're with them all the time so it might be a little harder for you to see. I know your kids aren't perfect, but Sean has manners and he respects his parents. Taylor is a lady. A little one, but a lady. I can see already that she is a caring person just like her mom."

Conrad interrupted, "You're right Peter, but what happened to that kid of yours?" The edges of Peter's mouth turned upward as Vince let out a deep chuckle. Vince watched Peter blush a little as he thought how appropriate it was that a little humor could indirectly be meant as a wonderful compliment.

"Here we go," Conrad said, focused on the TV. The screen had changed from a commercial to the inside of the Pontiac Silver Dome in Detroit.

"That commentator makes it sound like the Lions are going to go to the Super Bowl," Peter commented as all eyes in the room were now paying attention to the action on the screen.

"Not likely," Vince offered. "But it is Thanksgiving, Peter. Give those guys a break. This is their day. Most people can actually hope that Detroit wins." Vince pushed himself up. "Lori should have been here by now. I'll see if I can't get her on her cell."

"Good idea," Conrad nodded. "See if you can remember to leave a message this time."

"Thanks. It's always nice to have a supervisor."

After dialing, Vince listened as the phone made several attempts to connect. There was no success. Vince set the phone back in its cradle.

Melanie had heard her husband calling. "No luck?" She asked.

"Still no answer." Vince guarded his words carefully, knowing that others would be listening. "Lori probably turned her phone off. You know what I mean," Vince forced a smile as he stared right at Melanie.

"I'm getting better," Melanie defended herself, recognizing her husband was critiquing her own cell phone habits, also. Melanie was great at remembering to take her cell phone with her everywhere. The problem lay in that she most always failed to turn on the phone.

Melanie stepped from the hallway into the living room and placed her hand gently on Vince's. "Why don't you go and see if Dad's ready to come down. I thing that we will be sitting down to eat in just a little bit."

Lorraine was attempting to finish some last minute preparations. "Vince, Banner's shirt and pants are hanging in the closet. Let me know if you need any help."

"Sure Mom." And like a good son, he climbed the stairs to help his dad.

Chapter 17

As Vince walked up the stairs, his fingers squeezed the railing. His eyes focused on the tan carpet worn from years of foot traffic. On the last step, he stopped and hesitated. *This house has served my parents well.*

He looked down the hallway at the far bedroom which he had called his own for many years. In that room, he had done a ton of homework, dreamed about winning a bunch of games, listened to some really good music, and even read more than a few books. *Amazing, I still remember reading Catcher in the Rye in that room.*

The room had also witnessed a few tears. During his junior year in high school, he had wanted to use his parents' car to take Cindy Cooksey on a date. At that time, spending time with Cindy was the most important thing in his life, bigger than the next football game. For some insignificant reason, Banner said no. Vince remembered how he had begged and begged for his dad to reconsider, but to no avail. He stormed to his room, slammed the door, and threw himself on the bed. He cried like he had just lost a loved one and there would be no tomorrow. *That was not one of my better days.*

Vince sighed deeply. *It sure isn't easy being a parent.* He thought about how many times his parents had said no to him. They also had said yes a lot, yet for some reason, it was easier to remember the nos. *How interesting. It is probably more important for a parent to figure out when to say no than it is to say yes a hundred times.*

Vince pushed open the door to his parent's room and walked in. Banner was lying on his side with his eyes closed. His breathing seemed to be a bit labored, but sunshine peeking through the bedroom window glowed on the white comforter and gave the appearance that Vince's dad was at peace.

Quietly, Vince approached the closet. The four-paneled door squeaked the small squeak that Vince had heard a thousand times before as he turned the knob to the right. Just like Lorraine had said, a pair of pressed gray slacks hung next to a red and black checkered long-sleeved shirt that was obviously one of the owner's favorites.

Vince looked down the rod holding the clothes that Banner had regularly worn throughout his life. He reached out and ran his hands down the side of a dark blue suit with soft white pin stripes that he had seen Banner wear to church on a regular basis. It was the same suit he wore the day Vince graduated from the University of Toledo. Up above on the shelf were five or six sweaters. They were all professionally folded. *Mom's been to work in here.* A small gray box sat next to them. Vince did not need to look inside. He knew what the box held.

Two years ago he and Lori had convinced their parents to write out a living will so the whole family would know what Banner and Lorraine's wishes would be. At that time, no one would have thought that a grave situation could be staring them in the face on this Thanksgiving Day.

Besides the living will, Vince knew his father had stored all his valuable information in that box. Birth certificates, insurance policies, title to the car and truck, and even a few precious pictures of Banner, Lorraine, and their children. The box was sitting a little off center, so he gently pushed it back. As he looked down, he saw the evidence of one of his mother's guilty pleasures. All total, Vince was gazing at no less than three dozen pairs of shoes. *I'll bet Mom hasn't worn some of those shoes for years!* He turned his head and looked through the door as if his mom could have heard even his private thoughts.

He grabbed the pants and shirt and headed over to the bed. Banner had rolled over on his back and was watching his son move towards him.

"So you got stuck with the duty to clean me up." Banner whispered, trying to have his voice sound more forceful.

"I didn't get stuck with anything, Dad," Vince said. "Mom said I would get to eat your second helping of turkey and get an extra serving of pumpkin pie if I helped out."

"You haven't changed." Banner's voice sounded a little more powerful. "Your mother always knew that she could get to you through her cooking."

Vince helped Banner sit up and assisted him as he dressed for his journey downstairs. "Did Lori get in all right?" Banner questioned.

Putting his arm around Banner's shoulder, Vince forced himself to give a polished answer. "She should be here real soon." Then he used his best diversion skills. "There's a mighty big turkey waiting for you downstairs."

Chapter 18

As they approached the last step, Conrad sat up on the couch and tapped the side of the brown recliner. "Hey, Dad. Got the best seat in the house waiting for you. The Lions are even ahead by a touchdown."

Peter took his feet off of the ottoman and placed them on the carpet. "Uncle Banner, make that 10." All eyes focused on the TV as Banner slid into his recliner. "How long was that field goal?" Banner asked.

Before anyone could guess the announcer answered. "Make that a 43 yarder! He's made five in a row over the last three games!"

"Where are the boys?" Banner shifted his weight, trying to get comfortable.

"You have to ask a question like that?" Melanie asked as she walked into the living room and gave Banner a hug.

"I bet that game out back is better than the one we're watching in this room," Banner's grin made everyone feel at ease.

"One of you couch potatoes ought to go tell those boys that it is time to come in and get cleaned up," Melanie commanded.

"I can handle that," Peter said, pushing himself out of the sofa chair. As he started to walk across the room everyone heard the doorbell ring. "I got it." Peter veered towards the door.

The green door swung open revealing a circular vine wreath covered with brown and orange autumn decorations. "Well, hi, Pastor Lillibridge." Peter reached out to shake Nick's hand. "Mrs. Lillibridge, nice to see you," Peter said as he escorted the Lillibridges into the living room.

"Greetings my friend," Nick said, stepping to the side and letting his wife, Joanne, enter the Sanfords' home first. Joanne taught second grade at the Pleasant Street Elementary School. If someone had to pick people out of a line up and identify who was a teacher, Joanne would be the first one selected. Her caring eyes and endless smile gave everyone she met a sense of well-being. Pastor Nick loved to brag that Joanne could teach a rock to read.

Nick left little doubt that he worked for the Lord. His voice was endless in its ability to provide comfort to anyone who spoke with him and his eyes could reach deep into one's soul.

Everyone was now standing up, except for Banner. Vince was the last to welcome Nick with a sturdy handshake. "Good to see you, Nick. You must still be praying for me, because I still can't figure out how we beat Hilliard."

Nick's shake was firm and did its job. Vince felt a special moment of warmness that temporarily eased his concerns over Lori and his father.

"Thanks for the credit, Vince," Nick said with a smile. "But I suspect having an all-state quarterback didn't hurt, either." Nick slapped

Vince on the shoulder then turned to Banner. "How's my favorite usher?"

"I'm doing great. Nothing better than being with your family on a holiday," Banner said as he received his handshake. "Joanne please sit down. You take one of those soft spots on the couch next to Frank."

"Thanks Banner," she nodded at Frank. "I think I will see what Lorraine is doing in the kitchen." She grinned. "You boys don't need me messing up your ability to watch **another** football game."

Joanne peeked into the dining room on her way to the kitchen and admired the space. Lorraine knew how to make Thanksgiving special. The dining room table was set with place settings used only during holidays and other special occasions. A fall flower arrangement decorated its center. Normally about ten people could sit around the table, but today Lorraine had put in the extra leaf and twelve could now congregate comfortably.

Lorraine turned from the sink when she heard Joanne's voice. "The dining room looks beautiful, Lorraine. You haven't lost your touch."

"Why, thank you, Joanne."

"Smells mighty good in here," Joanne said, smiling at everyone in the kitchen.

"Should be ready in about ten minutes." Lorraine wiped her hand on her apron. "I've got a pretty good crew."

Barb spoke for the wives, "You know Lorraine, she's done most everything." Barb dropped a bar of butter into the pot of potatoes. "At least we get to mash the potatoes."

For the next few minutes the kitchen and living room were filled with holiday conversations. The women talked about what else needed to be done before dinner and sprinkled in comments about everyone's plans for Christmas while the men made conversation that would not solve any world problems and surely did nothing to help Detroit with their efforts to win the football game.

"She should have been here by now." Banner was the first to revisit Lori's absence. "Vince, why don't you try again?"

"Sure Dad." Vince grabbed his cell phone to speed dial his sister. The results were the same. No answer.

"Nothing, Dad."

"Lori's not here?" Nick asked. "She's always here before us." Nick stopped. It was clear he caught himself from going on. Everyone was reading Banner's face.

"Doesn't matter how old they get, Nick," Banner's exhale was noticeable. "You still worry about them."

"I bet she is pulling off of Interstate 71 right now." Nick tried to provide encouragement.

Everyone nodded, but no one knew for sure and no one had a better answer than to hope the pastor was right.

Lorraine stepped into the room. "Peter, didn't you forget something? Do you think you can break away from that game to go fetch those all-Americans in the back yard?"

"Oops, Vince you should have reminded me. Lorraine, if that means I am about to eat some of your fine cooking, it will be no problem." He headed to the back door.

Everyone in the house could hear him bark out his commands. "Your Grandmother said if you expect to eat any of her turkey and dressing, you better get in here right now!"

Four heads turned. They loved playing football, but the anticipation of a great meal captured their full attention.

Matt was the first one to reach the back door. "Can I have a drumstick?"

Conrad had walked into the kitchen. "My research shows that there are only two. Your chances are not real good!" Conrad slapped Sean on the back. "Make sure you march your teams to the bathroom. Chances are your moms might want some of that dirt off before we sit down to eat."

Walking through the kitchen the backyard heroes got welcoming smiles from the women who formed a passage as if they were conquering warriors. Lorraine embraced Matt as he passed and gave him a hug meant for all of her soldiers. "Yes, you can have a drumstick if that's what will make you happy today."

Their march ended at the bathroom. Sean was last in line. He stood in the hall across from the open stairway to the basement. He could hear his sister singing and playing, but Taylor must have been around the corner, because she was invisible to him. He could see the light switch not more than three feet from his hand. He hesitated, focusing on the noise from the game in the living room. He looked at the switch again. He knew Taylor was afraid of dark spaces. The temptation was too great. He flipped the switch.

He might as well have dropped an atomic bomb. The screams from the black basement were horrifying and heard by everyone within

100 yards, including his dad. "What's going on?" Vince shouted, as he ran towards the basement.

There was a thud and an even louder scream. Sean quickly reached for the light switch to flick it back on. He looked down the steps and saw Taylor on her knees, holding her head with both hands. Blood was trickling down the side of her face. When Taylor saw the blood, her sobbing just grew more intense.

Sean flew down the steps with Jay right behind him. "You okay?" Sean asked.

"Somebody shut out the lights." Taylor cried even louder.

Vince and Melanie were down the steps at the same time. They both had recognized Taylor's scream.

"Melanie, please get a wash cloth." Vince calmly pulled Taylor's hands away from her head. "What in the world happened?"

Vince could see a nice bump forming on Taylor's right forehead. The skin had cracked and the little blood seeping out was mixing with tears. He knew the feeling. Years ago he had loved to play hide and seek with his cousins in this basement and had been abruptly stopped on more than one occasion by one of the metal support poles. Banner seemed concerned the first couple of times, but later he figured the kids were just slow picking up on a powerful lesson: the pole always wins!

"Daddy, somebody shut the lights out on me," Taylor said, no sign of her tears letting up.

Melanie returned with a wet cloth and gently wiped Taylor's forehead. A crowd circled around her, all showing concern for the Dublin princess. Within a few seconds, the bleeding had stopped and Melanie kissed her daughter's head. "Come on, let's go upstairs and get a Band-

Aid for this. Your dad will find out who shut the lights out on you." She looked right at her son as if to say, "You just wait, mister."

"Any of you guys know what happened?" Vince asked.

He eyeballed the suspects. Jay looked at his cousin, Sean. Their eye contact gave Jay the notion that Sean had probably committed the act. "Uncle Vince, I don't know how it could have happened. Sean and I were just waiting to wash up in the bathroom. We didn't do nothing. I don't know what Matt was doing."

Matt was on the third step. "Hey, wait a minute. I was in the bathroom washing my hands." He was the only one with the perfect alibi.

Vince had been in these situations thousands of times as a dad and coach, with nobody wanting to confess. He now was trying to have eye contact with each of the four cousins. "Guilty" was usually written in a kid's eyes.

Before starting his investigation, Vince looked at the basement walls covered with grey paint. Once again, he was flooded with memories from his youth. The place was so familiar to him. The old concrete floor poured in the1950s. The old washing machine and dryer propped in the same position against the back wall. Banner's work bench, nestled into one corner, had the look of a vacant home wishing for the return of its owner. Lorraine's sewing machine sat on a four-legged table that probably had seen at least three generations of clothes spread across its surface. The ironing board stood right beside the table. It had seen more action than the sewing machine, but the iron looked brand new, and the safety light was on.

The southern wall had built-in shelves that held another relic from the past. Ball canning jars were filled with a variety of beans, corn, jelly, and some beets, among other things. All proof that Lorraine had stayed busy that fall.

That furnace looks good. Conrad, Lori, and he had all chipped in to buy their parents a new one three years ago. The water tank was not new, but it was a survivor. Although functional for the owners of the house, it rarely produced the hot water needed on holidays or other occasions when the rest of the family visited.

Vince remembered his bumps, his joys of playing with his friends and family in this rustic square footage. The memories were heartwarming, but it reminded him that Lori had still not arrived and he had an important matter to clear up and handle with the four boys standing at attention in front of him.

"All right, we are staying down here till I hear a confession from someone." Vince got four responses. Three from eyes looking right at him, and the fourth from eyes staring at the concrete floor.

Jay was the oldest and restated his position, "Sean and I were just waiting." He sneaked a smile again at his brother.

"Uncle Vince, I think Jay is trying to pin this on me. But, I swear, I was washing my hands." Matt's voice had the conviction of an innocent man.

"Don't look at me," Young Peter was very forceful. "Let's get the fingerprints off of the light switch."

"You've been watching too much TV," Jay protested. "This isn't *Law and Order.*"

"So none of you guys did it, huh?" Vince made an effort to scratch his head. "I guess Taylor did it herself?"

Sean had not said a word and his eyes had moved little from their focus on the basement floor. Vince knew his son. He wanted to give a little more rope. "Sean, how about you? You see one of your cousins flip the switch?"

It was clear from the expression on Sean's face that he had appreciated Jay's efforts to protect him, but living with his parents for fourteen years must have rooted some values. Honesty was one.

"Dad, I did it. I didn't realize that she would get hurt. Honest."

Sean was not able to finish his sentence. "Jay," Vince said. "Why don't you take these other guys upstairs? I would like to talk to Sean alone."

The three cousins did not wait for another command. They turned and sprinted to the top of the stairs. Jay closed the door.

"So you thought you would have a little fun with your sister?" Vince stiffened his back.

"Dad, it wasn't like that."

"Well, what was it like?"

"I was..." Sean's voice was silenced by his father's stern voice. "You thought that you would just have a little fun with your sister, at her expense." Vince put his hand on one of the metal poles. "These things don't give much." Sean's grimace let Vince know that he truly was sorry and that he wished he had never flipped the switch.

Vince tapped the pole two times. "Tell you what. Why don't you go to the other side of the basement and run full speed into this pole." Vince tapped the pole again for emphasis. "And I mean hit it with your hands behind your back. You know, so you get the full effect, like your sister."

Sean took one step towards the far wall, hesitated, "Dad, I can't do that, I'd knock myself out."

"You'll be fine. It didn't knock your sister out. You saying she's tougher than you?"

"No, I mean... you know... I could hurt myself." Sean muttered.

"When we get home, I will find something for you to do that will make your earlier choice have the right consequence." Vince could clearly tell that his son was remorseful about his actions. "For right now we will settle for an apology to your sister."

Vince walked halfway up the steps. He called, "Taylor, I need to see you." Melanie and Taylor had been waiting on the other side of the door when they heard Vine's command. Melanie's arm was wrapped around her daughter's shoulder as they started down the stairs. Taylor held a wet cloth against her forehead.

Melanie was the first to speak, "What are you two still doing down there?"

"I hope Dad is spanking him." Taylor said, as she rubbed her head. "I knew that Sean did it."

"Taylor, I said I needed to see you. You look all right to me. Come on down here."

Melanie lifted her arm and Taylor stepped closer to her dad, but she still wanted to send another volley at her brother. "Dad, he did it on purpose. I'm lucky that I'm alive."

"You're going to live. Get over here." Vince gently pulled Taylor to his side. "Let me see that." He took the cloth from its resting place. "Good job. It was the size of a golf ball. You got it down to a walnut."

Taylor placed her arm around Vince. "No thanks to him." Her voice carried the viciousness of a wounded victim.

Vince gave a little squeeze, reassuring his daughter that justice would be served. "I think Sean has something to say to you."

The brother and sister's eyes focused on each other. Sean coughed, then wiped the bottom of his nose. "I'm sorry. I mean… I really didn't mean to hurt you."

"Well you did. It hurts bad."

"Taylor, I said I was sorry," Sean pleaded, showing he thought his sister was giving him no credit or recognition for his apology.

"Daddy, you mean all he has to do is say he is sorry? You're not going to spank him? At least make him have to miss dinner." Taylor really did want to get even.

"How many times have I told you guys that there are choices and consequences?" Vince warmed up his preaching voice. "There is a time and place for everything. This is Thanksgiving and our family needs us to be around them, not fighting with each other."

Sean tried to capitalize on his Dad's comment. "Dad's right. Let's get upstairs."

"Not so fast Mr. Light Switch." Vince nudged Taylor over by her brother. He paused. His children stared back at him, not knowing what to do.

He thought about their ride up to Ashland, his conversation with his dad in the bedroom. His mom. Lori.

Was this one of those moments? Could he say something that would truly make a difference? Was it the Thanksgiving season that had made him feel so emotional about his family and his values? It really did not matter. He thanked God then turned his voice over to his heart. "Taylor, Sean knows that he will have to suffer the consequences of his actions."

Lowering himself into a kneeling stance he used thousands of times at football practice, his eyes looked upward at his most precious assets. "You know what I see?" He got no answer. Just a pair of puzzled glares. "I see a brother and a sister. And you know what? Life is not always going to be easy. This will not be your last conflict or disagreement, but, it was God's choice that you are brother and sister. No matter what happens in life, there will be no one who knows anyone better than the two of you will know each other."

Vince slid his hand through the side of his hair and over his ear. "Somehow you two need to figure out how to love each other and still respect the other's space and rights."

Sean grabbed his sister's hand. Taylor did not pull hers away. "I am sorry." Sean told her.

Vince stood up. "Let's go see if Grandad needs any help gettin' to the dining room table." He motioned for his children to head up the steps.

Melanie was waiting. "Well look who decided to come up and eat. Everyone else is about to sit down." She looked down at her daughter. "Did you get everything resolved?"

"Sean apologized," Taylor said, looking back. "I think he still has a chance at being a good big brother." Her words carried a smile.

Chapter 19

Vince was the last to walk into the dining room. Banner was at the head of the table and Lorraine was at his side. The rest of the family and the Lillibridges were standing, circled around the table and holding hands.

Lorraine asked, "Pastor Lillibridge will you bless this food?"

"It would be my pleasure." Nick nodded his head as the family gathered hands and bowed their heads. "Dear heavenly Father, We come together today in Thanksgiving for all you provide. We are thankful for this food set before us. Please let it nurture our bodies so we may perform your will. We are thankful for this home where we come together in loving fellowship. Let us continue to walk together through life's hills and valleys until you call us home to you. We are thankful for this family gathered round this table and those still traveling. Guide them safely to us." Nick paused and then continued, "Dear Father, we are thankful for the love of our dear brother, Banner. Lay your hands on him and heal him of the burdens his body is fighting. We are also thankful for the loving hands that prepared this meal set before us to help celebrate such a wonderful day. In your Holy name we give thanks."

Like a church congregation, everyone chimed in. "Amen."

Vince peered down at the table. Lorraine and the girls had worked another miracle. A huge stuffed turkey decorated the table. There was no shortage of side dishes. Green beans, baked beans, deviled eggs, and stuffing were ready to be served. A pan of broccoli rice casserole sat next to a generous bowl of mashed potatoes, yellow butter trickling down its top.

The center of the table was empty. The small candle arrangement that had been there only moments ago was now sitting on the side table with flowers and a few of Lorraine's special dishes.

Before anyone questioned the open space, Melanie focused on Lorraine. "All the kids, that's the grown up kids, too," she smiled at everyone. "Wanted you to have something special for this Thanksgiving." Vince picked up the pewter candelabra hidden under the table. Melanie caressed its solid base and presented it to Lorraine along with six scented candles.

"This is beautiful. What a sweet surprise. I love the candles. They smell like vanilla, my favorite." Her smile was genuine. So was Banner's.

Lorraine placed the candelabra in the center of the table. "Conrad, why don't you see if we can't find a match to set these aglow?"

"Mom, I don't think that will be a problem," Conrad reached into his pocket and pulled out a lighter.

Lorraine let everyone know it was time to experience the food that had been so lovingly prepared. "Everyone fix your own salads. The salad bar is set up in the kitchen. Grandkids first."

The grandkids ate at the kitchen table while the adults crowded around the dining room table. Amazingly there was rarely a fight at the grandkids' table, which was surely a result of the quality of food and lack of direct parental oversight. Their conversation normally centered on sports, some new TV show, or the latest electronics game.

Politics, religion, and more sports were popular subjects at the adults' table. Vince had a habit of asking a question that would start opinions flying.

Banner did not give Vince a chance to start the questioning. "Nick, thanks for mentioning Lori and Bonnie. It sure would be nice to know if they are okay."

Nick nodded agreement.

"I'm still sure they're all right." Melanie offered. "It just seems strange that we have not heard something. Lori loves to use her cell phone."

The coach in Vince clicked in. He had experienced problems, difficulties, and sudden changes throughout his coaching career. A turnover, a fumble, an interception, or a big penalty was nothing new to him. He would gather his players and let them know that everything was okay. They would be fine.

"Melanie is right. I'm sure she's well." He coughed, trying to toughen his voice. "She'd call if something was wrong." He looked across the table. "Dad, I sure am happy that you feel good enough to share dinner with all of us."

"Are you kidding? I feel great." Banner left no doubt he was willing that statement to be true. Everyone at the table could see the whiteness of skin, the fragile limbs, the draining effects that the villain cancer had taken on its victim. "What means so much to me is that our family could be together. That we could sit at this table and savor this food. Enjoy some special conversation."

Chapter 20

Vince cut a piece of his turkey and stared at his father. He did not say a word. Conrad made a comment, but Vince could not really concentrate and listen very well. His thoughts were centered around the frail condition of his father, his mother's pain, the soul-searching ride to Ashland, and the strange absence of his sister. He hoped that his dad knew how he felt. He hoped that Melanie knew how much being at this table meant to him. He hoped that his children would be touched the way that he had been. He hoped he was passing on his values like the man at the end of the table had done day after day. He hoped that his sister would call, or better yet walk through the front door.

Conrad's voice became clear, "Mom, what was your favorite Thanksgiving? I mean, number one all time. Which one would it be?"

"Oh Conrad, that's hard. You know we've had some good ones," Lorraine answered with a low voice that showed she liked the question, but it would take some time to figure out the answer.

"You know the one I remember most?" Peter spoke first. His voice forced everyone to listen. "When Conrad tried to beat Uncle Banner in arm wrestling." Peter looked at Banner and leaned back. "Come on Uncle Banner, you remember. We were sitting right in that living room."

Vince helped. "Conrad thought he could take Dad. What did it take? Ten seconds to pin him."

"Hey, I lasted a good 30 seconds!" Conrad defended himself.

Banner rolled his eyes, but they sparkled. "Got to admit, the boy looked solid as a rock across the table." Banner leaned forward. "I think it was the Thanksgiving that I had the flu. Only thing that I can think of to explain it taking so long to pin a young buck like yourself."

Smiles brightened the room. Vince stared at his dad. "You've been some rock yourself."

The silence that filled the room was not an uncomfortable silence. It was a respectful silence. Banner acknowledged the silence then motioned to his wife. "Hey, Lorraine never did say what her favorite was."

Lorraine winked at her husband. She was ready to share. "It was many, many years ago. None of you were there. My dad was a good but protective man He was never really ready to give away his little girl." She winked again at her husband. "But for some reason, Dad liked this skinny, brown-haired kid who kept coming over to the house asking if he could sit on the front porch with me or take me to a movie." Lorraine took a deep breath. Her eyes became dewy. "I was only nineteen and that kid was invited over to our house for Thanksgiving dinner. We had a full table, just like today. He didn't say much all through the dinner. Must have been nervous about something." Her lips showed a hint of a smile. "After dinner, almost everyone headed into the living room. Mom and Dad were still at the table. I looked at Mom and said

I needed to show her something in the kitchen. Now it was just the skinny kid and my father."

"The story goes that he tipped over his water glass, but he still asked the question." Lorraine deepened her voice. "Harry, I, I, I...I'd like to know if it is okay for me to marry your daughter?" Peeking over at Banner, she continued, "The next thing I knew we were standing alone at the bottom of the steps by the front door and Banner reached for my hand and pulled a ring from his pocket. I think he dropped it."

Lorraine waited for the table to finish their laughter, then spoke from her heart, "Honey, that was my best Thanksgiving and I have loved every one since then."

Banner reached his hand across the table and placed it on top of Lorraine's. Each person sitting at the table could sense the devotion each hand carried. The table was again struck by a moment of silence, another cherished moment with no words.

Vince continued to gaze at his parents and started selfishly asking why. He wondered why it had to happen. *His Dad did not deserve this fate. But, then who's allowed to pick their own fate?* His thoughts were cut off as Banner stood up slowly once more, then pulled his wife from the table.

"Honey, what are you doing?" Lorraine asked, as she willingly let herself be whisked away by her husband.

"We need a little music in here," Banner said with determined steps.

Vince watched his dad move over to the stereo player. Banner reached down into a stack of CDs, "This should work. Let's dance."

All heads were turned. By now, even the children in the kitchen could hear Alan Jackson singing "Remember When."

No one moved. They just watched as Banner took Lorraine into his arms and gently moved her across the floor. Jackson's voice echoed through the rooms.

The music stopped and the two lovebirds turned and walked back towards the table. Vince's thoughts moved from questioning to realizing how thankful he was that his dad was still here. That his mom was as beautiful as that Thanksgiving Day she took that engagement ring from his dad. Whatever lay ahead, they would handle as a family.

Chapter 21

Aglow settled over the house. Maybe it was the music, comforting food, or simply the conversation blossoming from family and friends together in the mood of Thanksgiving. It seemed impossible the mood could get better, but it did. There was a knock on the door. It swung open, seemingly on its own. Banner gently turned his head.

"Well, Dad, did you save us any turkey?" Lori stormed in with her boundless energy, Bonnie by her side. Lori began to tell the family about the accident they had witnessed on Interstate 71, while hugging everyone in sight. "Fortunately, no one was hurt, but traffic had been backed up for several miles. The accident happened in a construction zone, which made it even worse."

The children had left the kitchen and were clustered in the dining room behind the chairs, wanting to hear every word. Taylor and Bonnie exchanged happy hugs, then Lori stopped her story long enough to acknowledge the boys and put her arm around Taylor. "How're we doing guys?" She looked down. "Taylor, you look more like your mama every time I see you."

Vince could see that Lori was ready to continue her apology for being late, but Conrad was full of questions. "Why didn't you call? I know that you love that cell phone. You're on it all the time." Banner's laugh was the loudest.

Lori walked around the table and put her arms loosely around Vince's shoulders. He reached for her hand and kissed it, thankful she was safe. "What are the chances that from Cincinnati to Ashland there is probably only one dead spot? Go figure. The accident happened in that one dead spot."

Bonnie was quick to join in the banter. "Mom tried. I mean, she must have tried to call a thousand times." She looked at Lorraine. "Grandma, she knew that you would be worried sick." Bonnie smiled over at Conrad. "Hey, Uncle Conrad, did you teach Mom all those choice words she was using in the traffic jam?"

"Bonnie!" Lori stretched out her daughter's name.

"Not from me, sweetheart," Conrad smiled.

"Maybe I did say, gosh darn a few times." Lori threw her head to the side, then rushed back into her story. "Oh yeah, and the accident's not the end of it. Then my battery runs out! Can you believe it?" Lori stared right at Conrad. "And yes, I forgot my charger. Please don't lecture me on recharging." Lori's smile warmed everyone at the table. Banner and Lorraine's home was full of joy.

Vince reached up and squeezed his sister's hand. As he touched Lori's hand he thought about all the worry the house had held for several hours. And now it was as if the Lord had worked again in mysterious ways to make the family whole. The candles still burned brightly on the table. The turkey had been scattered about the plates. The coffee cups were full. The conversation moved from Lori's ordeal to the college games on Friday and Saturday. Vince looked across the room at his children, and then once again over at his parents and the rest of his family, and finally at Melanie. She returned his glance, seeming to understand his happiness as she always did.

Vince was experiencing something powerful. His soul was filled with Thanksgiving. He no longer was getting to Thanksgiving. He was there.

About the Authors

ALLEN BOHL

Dr. Allen Bohl is a native of Vermilion, Ohio. He earned a bachelor's degree from Bowling Green State University in 1970, a master's in education from the University of Southern Mississippi in 1973, and a Ph.D. from The Ohio State University in 1978.

His extensive career in athletic administration began as an Assistant Athletic director at The Ohio State University, then continued as Athletic Director at the University of Toledo, Fresno State, and the University of Kansas. For nearly 25 years, Bohl provided impressive leadership for athletic programs across the nation.

He is the author of *Back Porch Swing*, a heart warming story that speaks to the importance of faith, family values, character, and integrity.

Al and his wife, Sherry, live in St. Augustine, Florida where he is working on his third novel, *Over the Oak*…and playing golf!!

In addition, he is an adjunct professor at Flagler College and serves on the Community in Schools Board for St. John's County

They have two sons, Brett and Nathan, and a daughter, Heidi Sherwin. They are also the proud grandparents of four grandsons and two grandaughters.

BRETT BOHL

Brett Bohl is the Founder and President of The Bohl Group, Inc. - a consulting firm with a focus on fundraising, motivational speaking and direct sales, based out of Dublin, Ohio.

He is a dynamic leader, engaging speaker, and enthusiastic entrepreneur. Professionally, Brett has had the privilege to speak in front of numerous groups at the Corporate, Government and University levels.

Before leaving the corporate world to start his own company in the spring of 2004, Brett worked in the Educational Software, Technology Consulting and the Executive Search and Recruiting Industries, achieving multiple awards and recognition.

He is a graduate of The University of Toledo where he played football for The Rockets and was an active member of Beta Theta Pi Fraternity.

Brett and his wife Joyce have been blessed with two children – son, Brady Allen and daughter, Taylor Lorraine

To request Allen or Brett for a signing
or speaking engagement please visit
WWW.ALLENBOHL.COM or E-MAIL,
BOHLBOOKS@BELLSOUTH.NET